I0683430

Writer's Digest Self-published Book Award Judge's Commentary:

The old, Wild West comes to life in **Last Chance**. Who wouldn't love a cover featuring a sunset with the sun in the shape of a pool ball? I had to smile when I picked this one up. And, after reading it, I was still smiling long afterwards. A strong, witty writing style kept me turning the pages. No plot holes were noted and I was so absorbed by this one that I finished it in one sitting. Mystery, humor, and a fun cast of characters make this one a top-notch find for me.

The author's voice is definitely strong and well-suited for the genre. It was difficult to find any suggestions for improvement here. Really, no major issues of note. I think the cast was the perfect size. I think the pacing was perfect, in fact, it almost ended too soon for me. A great mix of narrative and dialogue kept me hooked from chapter to chapter. A nice resolution left me satisfied, yet I hope that this author continues on with the series. . . . But really, this was just a fun read from cover to cover.

Writer's Digest awarded Mose Duane the National Self-Published Book Award's Certificate of Merit for **The Billiard Guidebook** (A Rookie's Guide to Pool Table Maintenance and Repair).

Testimonials

Last Chance is as good as if not better than anything else you will read this year.
— Curtis C., Indianapolis

I cannot believe this is a first novel. Excellent work from Mr. Duane.
— Kevin J., Charlotte

Damn good! What more can I say?
— Sissy O., NYC

I love to read first novels. They are usually quirky and fun. *Last Chance* by Mose Duane did not let me down. It is an original, fun, and fast read. I Loved it.
— Jerry P., Phoenix

If you want to spend a delightful evening reading, you can't go wrong with any of Duane's books, including *Last Chance*. It's a terrific read.
— N.Y.T., New York

Also by Mose Duane

A Rookies Guide to:
Pool Table Maintenance and Repair
Buying or Selling a Pool Table
Playing Winning Pool
Pool Table Assembly

Novels:
Last Chance (JC's Last Chance)
Coyote Stands
Something Substantial
The Great Pool Table Heist of Arizona
      (Obama and the Dixie Chicks)
Bigg Dick: Real Justice
Pussy Willows: A Bigg Dick Novel

Available
All of Mose Duane's books are available
online at amazon.com and kindle, b&n.com and
nook, Apple Books, Google Books, Kobo, and
major booksellers through Books-in-Print.

About the Author

Mose Duane has written four **A Rookie's Guide to** billiard books and four novels. He lives in Arizona with his lovely wife Karen.

Like him on Facebook.com/MoseDuane.

LAST CHANCE

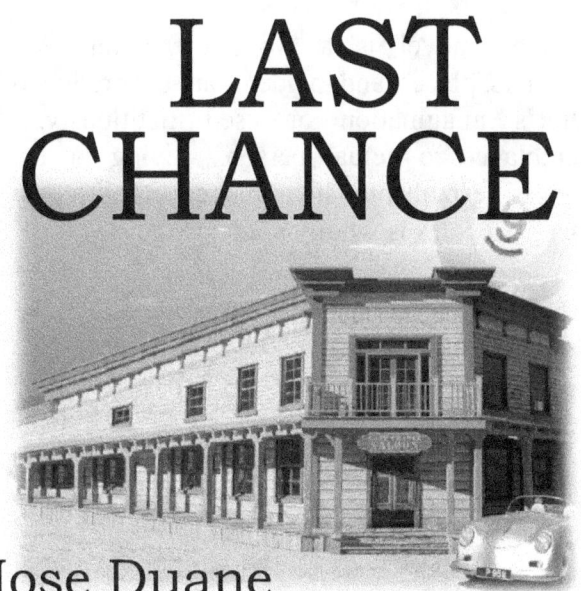

Mose Duane

www.phxbilliards.com

This novel is a work of fiction. Names, characters, places, and incidents are the product of the author's imagination or used fictitiously. Any resemblance to actual persons—living or dead—business establishments, images, artists, events, cities, or locales is wholly coincidental.

Cover designed by the author

ISBN 979-8823155649
2nd edition
ISBN 978-0669808918

Acknowledgment

Thanks to friends and family members who took the time to help me make this book possible. A special thanks to my amazing daughters for their encouragement and insight.

Ya got trouble,
Right here in River City!
With a capital T
And that rhymes with P
And that stands for Pool.
We've surely got trouble!
Right here in River City!

—Robert Preston - Music Man

One

Midmonth, October 10, 2015, Tony "J.C."
Forkner carefully and deliberately funneled the fine-
grained blasting powder into the narrow crack around
the perimeter of the safe's door, packing it in as tight as
possible with the edge of a wooden coffee stirring stick.
He then forced a six-inch fuse into the powder at the
bottom of the door and hoping he'd used enough to do
the deed he lit the fuse and ran like hell from the room
slamming the door shut behind him. The blast, though
muffled somewhat within the confines of the small
office at the back of the Velvet Rail Family Billiard
Center, shook the building, rattled the windows, and
sent him stumbling over his own feet, face first onto the
floor.

"Christ!" he mumbled as his chin hit the unyielding
surface, "Christ O Mighty."

Dense black smoke poured from the crack below
the office door engulfing him, causing an involuntary
coughing spasm. He paused, sprawled on the brick
patterned linoleum, listening for distant sirens in case
some lost soul had heard the explosion and called the
law. He was certain, however, that no one of
consequence would be within earshot that early in the
morning, even with a noise as thunderous as the one he
had created.

After a couple of minutes, he pushed himself up.
His knees wobbled and his hands shook from pure

exhilaration of such a bold move, far beyond anything he'd ever done. He wiped at the black soot covering his white cotton work trousers and tee shirt, only to produce dark smears. "Christ," he said again, "Christ O Mighty."

Gingerly he made his way through the small and now murky hallway to the snack bar at the front of the poolroom. From beneath the counter, tucked behind paper cups and packets of napkins, he pulled out a bottle of Wild Turkey 101, Kentucky's finest liquid nerve. The family aura of the Velvet Rail, owned and operated by an old man named Johnny Bishop who insisted on calling it a *family* billiard center and adamant about the appearance of a clean and legal establishment, had always compelled J.C. to keep his bottle well hidden, until now. Now it simply didn't matter. He parked himself at the counter, poured a tall glass of the whiskey, knocked it back, and poured another. Waiting for the smoke to dissipate into the air conditioning ductwork, and for his substantial surge of adrenalin to subside, he propped his grimy, bearded face up with trembling hands, his nose hovering only inches above the wide glass of whiskey. "Christ," he muttered again, this time into the glass, "Christ O Mighty," and the liquid rippled sending up the delicious, pungent aroma of bourbon whiskey that always brought a smile to his face, and he smiled. He knew he should be scared shitless, having no doubts that he would go to jail or shot pointblank for what he'd just done, but he smiled.

From his shirt pocket, trapped behind a now flattened pack of smokes, he retrieved a note, unfolded it, and laid it on the countertop. His wife had written the note on a sheet of yellow school paper, and his thirteen-year-old son, Kid, had given it to him only an hour earlier. She had dropped Kid off at the side entrance of the Velvet Rail before she left town, yet again. They had an on again off again marriage, had been separated for more than two weeks this time, so J.C. was certainly surprised to see the boy waiting for him when he came in for early morning cleanup duty, and even more surprised to see the busted side entrance door. Kid was wearing the same ragged shorts and striped tee shirt he'd been wearing the last time J.C. had seen him. He was also still carrying the same old child's Batman backpack with a fainted yet visible caricature of the Joker on the back, which was a startling reminder to J.C. of how near destitute they actually were.

J.C. had read the note as soon as Kid handed it to him. After he read it, with no preplanning or thought of consequences—good or bad—he knew what he had to do. He'd quickly emptied the backpack, sent the boy off to school with his supplies in a paper bag, and waited just long enough for the boy to be out of hearing range before retrieving the blasting powder and blowing Johnny Bishop's safe to smithereens.

J.C. picked up the half-empty glass of bourbon, took a sip, and again read the note from a wife half his age, a wife who had grown up in an affluent family, but had taken on the qualities of a pool hall junkie in just a few years.

Tony

Early this morning Rabbit and I stole all of Johnny Bishop's pool cues and hocked them to Stony over at his pawn shop. Although they're probably worth 4 or 5 times as much he gave us $2500 for them. We decided to take the money on the road first to Johnston City and then Rabbit thinks I've got the stroke and I know I've got the passion to be a good enough player to bankroll us on up to Chicago and on to the big time. Rabbit also thinks I'm wasting my time hanging with you anymore since you'll always work for Johnny at the pool hall and will never go on the road again yourself. So I guess that means I'm leaving you for good this time. I'm putting Junior in your care for the time being because he's still in school and he would slow Rabbit and me down anyway. Make sure he brushes his teeth and gets to school on time. I will always love you.

Blondie

Rabbit, the long and greasy haired, pot smoking kind of fixture of any pool hall in the country, was always hanging around the Velvet Rail, always ready for a game, and always ready to make a play for any bimbo gullible enough to listen to his come-hither drivel. Even though he could smoke two joints and still be subject to run three straight racks for a sawbuck, he would never be serious enough to be a top player, not as J.C. could've been, had he not knocked up Blondie, had he not found the liquid version of Rabbit's joints: good old Kentucky bourbon.

Back in the day, when J.C. was clear-headed, serious, sensible, committed, and fearless, he could—and did—beat anyone who came down the pike. It didn't matter the game—One Pocket, Nine Ball, Eight Ball, Straight Pool, Bank—he was the master of the green. They called him J.C. after all because he'd won most every pool tournament from here in L.A. to Houston and from Tijuana to Vegas shooting pool like Jesus Christ himself. He did so while using an original ivory tipped Rambow cue as his scepter of power. The fact that he'd won the Rambow up in Vegas off a dark-skinned white man, who in no way resembled a reasonable person, and still walked around to talk about it just added to the mystique of his pool-shooting prowess. The dark-skinned man's name was Levi Berry but was called Black Berry by most.

J.C. swiveled on his stool and looked around the poolroom. It was now eerily quiet except of course for the sound of the boom still ringing in his ears. There was also a faint mist of smoke and soot yet lingering, and a slight persistent odor of the five-year-old blasting powder he'd taken from Johnny Bishop's storage shed, but nothing that would give him away even if some misfit pool player were to wander in. The blasting powder, a compound of nitrate, sulfur, and charcoal, was left over from back when Johnny Bishop fancied himself a gold miner, as did most old timers who visited California's Sierra Nevada Mountains on a regular basis.

J.C. had always thought of the Velvet Rail as a nice place, for a pool hall. The pool room itself, separated from the snack bar by a half wall, consisted of an ample carpeted expanse of twenty-five pool tables arranged every other one perpendicular to the next, not a typical one row of four or six tables. It was never busy that time of morning, even when Johnny had tried the open-twenty-four-hours-a-day thing a couple of years back. Come evening though, the room would fill with hustlers and wannabe hustlers, male and female, young and old, rich and poor, clear heads and pot heads—a simmering cauldron of social classes and races, J.C. often thought, boiling up at times, but never quite erupting.

On the far wall—the wall of records as it was gratuitously referred to—hung pictures of local players who'd done magnificent things on a pool table. A picture of Johnny was there, from when he was a young man and could beat anyone in the Southwest, black, white, brown, or red—as Johnny himself would put it. A picture of J.C. leaning on his Rambow after beating Rabbit in a One Pocket game was there too. He'd sent Rabbit to his hole somewhere along the ransacked streets of south L.A., before he came back to lay Blondie over the hood of his car and fill her with thoughts of grandeur, among other things. There was also a picture of her, the beautiful two-month pregnant pool-shooting champ, from when she won the North Vegas championship thirteen years back.

J.C. swooped up his whiskey glass, put it to his mouth and made sure it was now equivalent to how he felt about his life: empty. He wadded up the note and threw it at the picture of the beautiful two-month pregnant pool-playing champ.

"Christ O Mighty," he said to the picture. "You know I'll always love you too . . . how do I merit such misery from you?"

He pushed himself from the stool, wobbled to the wadded note that had flopped to the floor without ever reaching the picture, picked it up and shoved it back into his pocket not wanting to leave any evidence of Blondie's wrongdoing. Behind the counter, he poured himself another full glass of Kentucky courage.

Sadly, the pool cues Blondie and Rabbit absconded with did not belong to Johnny Bishop. If that were the case, J.C. would simply arrange with Johnny to work off the debt, having no doubt that Blondie would be back one day. Instead, as his luck would have it, the cues belonged to Levi Berry, alias Black Berry, who had for reasons unknown showed up in L.A. two years after losing the Rambow to J.C. A couple of weeks after that he had sucked Johnny into a three-sided Nine Ball game with him and a "stranger from up north." Johnny couldn't pay off his losses, so Black Berry settled for the right to sell all pool cues at the Velvet Rail in perpetuity. Indirectly, becoming a backroom business partner for life unbeknownst to most casual observers, including Blondie or surely, she would never have crossed him. Being a short, but well-proportioned and handsome man did not stop the rumors that Black Berry would hurt people over business or self-gratification on occasion depending on circumstances. It was also believed by most that he packed a pistol, knew how to use it, and that his services were once utilized from as far north as Reno to as far south as Mexico City.

Black Berry kept the supply room well stocked with top brand pool cues like Vikings, Meuccis, Schons, Balabushkas, and even a couple of old thousand-dollar Hoppes, and Josses; and offered weekly payments at not so reasonable interest rates. Still, using the Velvet Rail as a front, he sold a "shit-pot" full of cues from San Diego to Vegas, and no one with an ounce of sense ever missed a payment.

J.C. was confident Black Berry would never believe that Blondie and Rabbit could mastermind such a feat of stealing and fencing his pool cues on their own and would therefore take out his aggression in a spectacularly painful manner on him or Kid, or both. So, he reasoned, if you were going to be accused of robbery you might just as well rob something and take everything while doing so. Moreover, though not common knowledge, it was certainly no secret that Black Berry kept his cash stashed in Johnny Bishop's safe.

J.C. carefully worked the glass of bourbon up and in two gulps half emptied it again. "Christ," he said mumbling. "Jesus H Christ." In the not-too-distant past, he'd held the conviction that the solution to life lie in cue-ball positioning, one shot progressing to the next without hooking yourself, giving you the ability to win game after game after game. If you could control that single two-and-a-quarter-inch sphere, you had life by the balls, so to speak.

But now, overweight, graying, and with most of his forties behind him, he was finding more and more miscues, more and more hooks, more and more pocket rattling, ball rejecting tit shots that could not be interpreted as purely chance. And the years had bestowed to him eyes that refused to focus long enough to make a cut shot of any respectable angle, and hands that only stopped trembling after a quick knockback of Kentucky's finest. That calamity of old age and liquor led to his being pounded by a host of young guns, wanting not necessarily his glory, his cue stroking godliness, but certainly his last Washington. And that leading to this absurd, humiliating job at the Velvet Rail Family Billiard Center, and a wife that would put his life in the hands of a madman for a handful of miserable pool cues and a roll in the sack with a young dicked, long-haired hippie called Rabbit.

With the building now void of lingering smoke, with his nerves settling into a more usual state of intoxication, J.C. pushed himself away from his drink, and staggered back to the office where Johnny Bishop's safe once stood. He shoved hard on the office door to clear a path into a room that was now a blackened heap of upended office fixtures. The safe's twisted door was firmly embedded into the side of Johnny's solid oak desk. "Christ O Mighty," J.C. said as he surveyed the upheaval. Although impressive looking, the safe had been bought at a big box store for cheap and had come apart at every seam, like dropping a cherry bomb into a Coke can, with what he'd thought were just a few grams of blasting powder.

Some smoldering packets of money were strewn about, but most of the bills had scattered completely, covering every inch of the room. Methodically, he began gathering up random denominations and stuffing them into Kid's backpack, showing a preference for Franklin and Grant, and even Jackson if not severely scorched or torn. He held total disregards for all the other presidents, leaving those in shredded pieces littering the room.

With every nook, cranny, and pocket of the backpack stuffed with bills, with the Joker's face stretched to its grotesque limits, J.C. was astonished as to how much money had been in the safe, far more than the daily sales of a couple of pool cues would bring, he was sure. He smiled again, large and bold this time, at the magnificent haul as he slung the hefty backpack over one shoulder.

10

Back at the snack bar, he raised the half empty glass of whiskey to Blondie's picture, "One hell of a hook shot, my love," he said then emptied the glass in one long swallow. He picked up the bottle of Wild Turkey, tucked it under his arm, and walked out of the side door, the one she and Rabbit had broken through much earlier that morning.

Two

Six years earlier, Levi Berry drifted into California by way of Johnston City, Illinois and then Las Vegas, Nevada. Levi won big at the annual Johnston City pool hustler's tournament where pool players' dreams and opportunities were more often trampled than realized. He didn't win the tournament itself, which consisted mostly of young players who fancied themselves as potential tour players. They were there essentially to get their names out to the public with aspirations of snagging an appearance on one of the many sterile televised events, and from that, picking up a sponsor or two. Levi won his money in the much more lucrative no holds barred backroom aftergames where there were more C-notes in the pool table pockets than balls, and where two strangers could trap a gifted but unsuspecting rookie player and fleece him of his bankroll in short order. After Johnston City, Levi had no intention of going to Vegas. He simply followed the pool players and their money.

Levi had no real knowledge of his heritage other than having some Cherokee blood from a distant past, but figured he had the good fortune of being born with russet eyes, dark curly hair, light brown skin (chocolate in the summer months), and a small frame. He quickly discovered he could pass for Negro, Mexican, or Caucasian depending on the configuration of his clothing and facial hair, which usually involved western attire—including Tony Lama boots and Stetson hat—a thin cut moustache, and a clean-shaven jaw. He also kept himself in reasonable shape—muscular chest, arms, and flat stomach—more for self-preservation than vanity, but it didn't bother him that women adored it, especially the heavy-duty ones. Nor did it bother him that some men also found him attractive. He wasn't particularly prejudiced.

It was also his good fortune that some pool players, especially those who frequented backstreet pool halls and bars, were inclined to believe any hackneyed stereotypical yarns put to them about other groups. The erroneous belief that blacks were excellent pool players, whites were mediocre, and Mexicans were lousy, worked very much to his advantage. When he played the role of an inebriated overconfident black, a sloppy Mexican, or a cocky white, the respective suckers just couldn't help themselves, and kept his bankroll expanding faster than a banker's dream.

While in Vegas, Levi took on the persona of a Mexican tough guy, carrying a heavy but highly effective semiautomatic Colt .45 caliber pistol that he'd purchased at an army surplus store. He tried on several occasions to find a link to the Vegas underground, Mafia, crime syndicate, or whatever it was called—he had no idea— but couldn't find anyone who knew anyone with a connection. However, he did stumble onto a couple of well-to-do thugs and small casino owners who paid him generously to control card counters, chip counterfeiters, excessive winners, cheaters, and other undesirables. Two of the chip counterfeiters from Jersey were still buried in the desert, as far as he knew, each with a single .45 caliber hole in his heart.

Levi left Vegas shortly after Juan Hernandez introduced himself with ten-grand in cash. Juan said he was a member of the Mexican drug cartel, had heard of Levi and his talents, and wanted him to take care of a Guatemalan named Marco Perez who was ratting to the FBI, CIA, ICE, or some agency of equal importance, of the locations of shared smuggling routes and distribution channels down in San Diego. Juan Hernandez sweetened the deal by promising another five grand upon completion of the job.

Marco Perez, however, proved to be crafty and managed to escape across the border as Levi emptied his pistol at him. But Levi was so sure that he scared Perez so deep into the underbrush of Mexico, or maybe all the way back to Guatemala, that no one would ever question whether or not the guy was dead and buried.

He'd chased Perez to the U.S. Mexico border fence where he dug into the loosely packed dirt, then pulled up a round wooden manhole size trap door. Levi managed to fire three rounds as Perez disappeared into the ground, and when he popped up on the other side of the fence, Levi emptied the 45 at him. But, like some terrified desert rat, he bobbed and weaved through the brambles without so much as a bullet hole in his flapping shirt.

Levi decided that there was no way he was going to go back to Vegas and face Juan Hernandez, or any of his possible associates, and confess his failure, the five-grand bonus be damned. How was it his fault, he reasoned, that the Mexican was stupid enough to give him ten-grand in cash up front?

Consequently, Levi ended up in L.A. as a black pool hustler calling himself Black Berry. He quickly took to the L.A. scene where the easy to beat pool players and the almost constant sunshine were a dream come true for him. The brilliant California sun gave him the dark skin he needed to pass as a black man, and he now spent at least an hour everyday poolside to maintain his deception.

Today, two years after the hit on the Guatemalan went awry, Juan Hernandez unexpectedly appeared in L.A. at Black Berry's apartment door as he returned from the swimming pool. Black Berry was in trunks and towel, without a weapon, when Juan emerged from the shadows, slipped behind him, and slammed his face into the door before he could open it.

"Hey *hombre*," Juan growled in a forceful whisper and vigorously pressed the side of Black Berry's face into the door, smashing one eye against the wood doorframe and forcing the other to cock sideways, "you have stole our *dinero,* and make me look bad in front of my *compadre*."

"You paid me to get rid of the scumbag from Guatemala. That's what I did." Black Berry managed to squeak out the words from the side of his mouth.

We pay you to bury him. You did not. Now he is back. This too is greatly embarrassing for me in front of

15

my *compadre,*" Juan pushed so hard that Black Berry felt his vertebrae pop.

"Tell me where the fucker is," Black Berry whined, "and I'll take care of it."

"It has been taken care of by someone else. Now we want our *dinero* back, and I too can return to *México* without humiliation."

"I don't have it," Black Berry said and considered the value of rushing into the apartment to grab his pistol. The door key was already in the lock. All he had to do was turn it and shove, but he'd had no way of knowing if the Mexican was alone, so he'd stood with his face wedged against the door like some prized idiot.

"We are not stupid like you, *amigo*. We know where it is kept at the pool hall. We could go there and take it if we choose. That would maybe bring unwanted notice to us here in the U S of America, so we would prefer to deal with only you, and you will not disappear again, unless we make it so. *Comprendes*?"

Then Black Berry felt the cold blade of steel push against his exposed ear, and a trickle of blood ran down his jaw.

"This is my way of getting your *atención*," Juan said. "Next time I cut it off. Maybe I also cut off your *testículos*."

"*Comprende, comprende*," Black Berry yelled as he felt the blade slide between his legs. And seeing no way out, he pleaded for mercy and promised to give the money back in return for keeping the admirable parts of himself.

"Just give me a couple of days and don't do anything rash."

"Mañana." Juan twisted the knife.

"Son of a bitch be careful, please," Black Berry pleaded. "I'll get it."

"Mañana, yes," Juan repeated.

"Yes, tomorrow."

"Plus interest maybe, to make everyone happy."

"Plus interest. Of course."

Three

J.C. had tossed the cash laden backpack into the trunk of his car and driven to Johnny Bishop's home where he knew Kid would be, instead of school. He slid his old "shit-brown" weather beaten Honda Civic to a dusty stop barely missing the stoop at the front door and wondered if the car still had enough guts for the journey in front of it. The seat, worn threadbare from years of use by a previous owner or two before Blondie bought it from Stone's Pawn Shop more than a year back, squeaked loudly in defiance of his weight, and the front tires squealed from need of alignment. The CUE BALL license plate was its only redeeming feature. One of Blondie's few good ideas, as far as he was concerned.

Johnny's house was within walking distance of the Velvet Rail, but few walked. Johnny had purchased the then beautiful little house, with white picket fence and all, over forty years earlier for his wife, who died shortly thereafter of "God knows what," according to Johnny. Now the house, in dire need of repairs and paint, looked bleak and misplaced in an otherwise tidy neighborhood. The picket fence had been torn down long ago to make room for parking in what used to be a manicured front yard.

Johnny looked up from his pool table, formed a V with two fingers, and put them to his lips as J.C. walked in. Johnny's unbuttoned, loose fitting shirt exposed sagging, grayish skin with little hair. In his youth, he'd been called Red, but the years had bleached all traces of auburn from his hair and freckled skin leaving the gray wash of protracted death. He'd just missed a combination shot involving three balls. "Well, Eddy, that'll cost me a C-note, for sure," he said to his opponent, sounding irritated. Because every pool hustler worth his moniker knew that combination shots involving three or more balls were bait shots, sucker shots, or showoff shots, depending on how they are used, J.C. figured the old man had more than likely missed on purpose.

Eddy carried a new top end cue. He wore creased dress pants and a light blue shirt with no coat or tie. J.C. didn't recognize the guy or the cue. He was either a sucker trying to look like a hustler or a hustler trying to look like a sucker. Johnny couldn't tell the difference anymore.

They were playing on Johnny's mid-1900, nine-foot Brunswick Gold Crown and had frozen a thousand each. After twenty games, they would tally up the wins and losses then divide the money accordingly. Johnny had restored the table himself. He'd dismantled a wall between the living and dining rooms of the small house to accommodate it. Though the floor now sagged beneath its weight, Johnny managed to keep the table perfectly level and flawlessly green. He preferred all high stakes games to be played on it in private and away from the Velvet Rail. J.C. had won and lost a grand or two on the table himself.

J.C. pulled out his pack of Lucky Strikes, shook out two flattened cigarettes, placed one between his teeth, handed the other to Johnny, and lit both with a two-inch flame from an old butane lighter.

"You been drinking?" Johnny asked. "You seem mighty nervous, and look at you, you're covered with filth."

Kid was lounging on a sofa thumbing through a Playboy magazine he'd found on the coffee table and without looking up said, "Christ, Johnny, of course Pop's been drinking, duh!" Kid was an odd name for a youngster. J.C. had always thought so, but neither he nor Blondie gave him the name. The boy had been called Junior until some genius lost fifty dollars in a game of Eight Ball to the then ten-year-old. The genius then decided he was just like his father so started calling him Kid J.C. The name had since been shortened simply to Kid. Kid was now patiently waiting for Johnny to be done with his current contest. The old man wanted to demonstrate the wonders of reverse english to him, though J.C. was sure Kid already had the concept mastered. J.C., Blondie, and Johnny had been teaching him the subtleties of the game since he was old enough to sit on the table and roll the balls into the pockets.

J.C. frowned at Kid, but wished he had a drink. He'd thought about leaving town without the boy, had been thinking about such a move since receiving the note from Blondie. He was sure the school or Johnny would eventually take care of him or see to it that someone else did. Hell, he thought, the kid would be much better off in a foster home rather than tagging along with someone most likely destined to be shot without notice. "Put the porn down and get your stuff!" he said snapping more loudly than he wanted to. "I guess I'm taking care of you now, so we gotta go." Then, in a calmer voice, he told the old man about Blondie and Rabbit taking the pool cues, leaving the boy for him to look after, and how he'd then felt compelled to turn the safe into a pile of scrap iron.

"She and that worthless bum busted down the side door and took all of Black Berry's cues, so you then decided to also take his money." Johnny summed up the situation as if he couldn't believe what he'd heard.

"Wow," Kid said, "that means both you *and* mom are now criminals."

J.C. scowled. "The boy needs his mother," he said. "I can't take care of him, and you know it." Beads of sweat covered his face. Johnny liked to keep the room dreadfully hot; it made everyone but him uncomfortable.

"If that son of a bitch catches you," Johnny said, "you're all worm food so it won't matter."

"I'm going to use the money to find her, and Black Berry will be broke. I don't see how he can follow us very far."

"He'll follow you all right," Johnny replied. "You have his money. He'll be on you like flies on shit even if he has to walk."

"Are we on the lam now, Pop?" Kid asked.

J.C. pointed to the door. "Go get in the car."

"Mom said for me to stay with you because she'd be on the lam."

"What else did she say?"

Kid pinched his nose. "That you'd get drunk too, and—"

"Didn't need no magical eight-ball for that one, kiddo. You said it yourself."

"She also said you might shoot yourself, that you had a gun in the car. But I don't think she knew you were going to blow up Johnny's safe and take all of his money."

"It's not Johnny's money . . . and what would I do with you if I shot myself?"

"Yeah, I know. Sometimes mom makes no sense at all," Kid answered with a shrug and a smile, and then ambled toward the front door with his paper bag of school supplies. "But I think we're on the lam now too, just like mom," he said over his shoulder as he let the door slam shut.

With round, deep crevassed lips, Johnny took a long drag of the Lucky Strike and watched the boy meander to the car. He pulled the smoke deep into his lungs and let it billow from his nostrils. He was old but looked ancient. His profoundly wrinkled skin drew tight to the bone. "For sure," he said, "I know a boy needs a mother, but I'm not sure he needs that one, not anymore."

"Yeah," J.C. said, "but I need her."

"No, you'll get along without her, once you get used to the idea, so you don't need to go traipsing across the country looking for her. You'd be better off if you took the boy and just disappeared."

"Are we going to play, or what?" Eddy quickly spoke after running most of the rack and then dogging an easy cut shot trying to pull the cue-ball back for an impossible position play on the nine-ball. "And who the hell is Black Berry? You guys talk about him like he's some kind of a gangster."

Johnny gave him a hard, dead stare. Eddy slumped, walked to a spectator's chair by the window and leaned into it, his blue shirt dulled by sweat.

"Hell bub, I forgot you were even here," Johnny said, "and that sorry son of a bitch will shoot your young ass too, gangster or not, so don't you go repeating anything you've heard here, understand?"

"Man, I didn't hear anything," Eddy said, "nothing."

"She didn't know they were Black Berry's cues, did she?" Johnny turned and asked J.C.

J.C. gazed into the old man's pale eyes. "I don't think so; she never paid much attention to what goes on around here. But Rabbit should have known."

"Yeah, that son of a bitch knew all right. And he knew what Black Berry was capable of and that's why he ran like a cat with its ass on fire, dragging her along with him," Johnny said. "But she thought they belonged to me. All I've done for you and that girl—" he shook his head "—that's just plain screwed up. And you say Stony has the cues now?"

"That's what the note said . . . that they sold them to Stony."

"Well, he's a dead man walking that's for sure, strung up by his balls probably, and gutted like a pig. And you knew Black Berry would make headcheese out of you over the cues too, even though you had nothing to do with it, so you went ahead and snatched his money." Johnny shook his head, again summing up the situation, still trying to get a grip on what had happened.

"From the beginning, yeah, I knew I didn't have a choice."

"Well hell, J.C., you know he'll be here soon enough," Johnny said, "and he'll be on the goddamn warpath."

"Kid and I'll head for Bayfield to stay clear of him, and to see if Blondie went up there to visit her folks. If she's not there, then we'll probably head for Chicago."

The old man pointed a skeletal finger toward the door. "Well, whatever you do, you'd better get the hell out of here while you can—" his eyes watered and his voice cracked "—and don't ever come back, hear me . . . none of you."

"What about you?" J.C. asked. "You know he'll be pissed at everyone, including you."

"I'll be fine. He knows I wouldn't screw with him, so I don't think he'll bother me either." Johnny turned to Eddy, "You were just purely unlucky missing that shot there, comrade," he said, "just plain ol' unlucky. Hell, you had it won."

Then, pretending as if nothing of consequence had happened, as if he would never miss J.C. and the boy, as if they were never part of his life, he proceeded to run out the table to go three games up.

Four

Black Berry dangled his legs over the wrong side of his bed right at ten o'clock, his head hammering in thundering pulses of boom, boom, boom with the rhythm of his heartbeats. If only he had the self-control to follow his own simple rule—no alcohol while working—his life would run in a much smoother fashion. Taken without the stupefying drinks, his body could tolerate moderate drugs like marijuana, cocaine, or LSD with no noticeable morning side effects, but mix in two or three drinks and his mind became a pounding playground of distant drums.

The bed moved as someone shifted. The distinct odor of a heavy woman stirred up recollections of what had occurred the night before. This one happened to be white, but it didn't matter—white, black, brown—to him, they all had that same smell of too much powder and perfume in places where bathing could be difficult; an odor that always brought about memories of his mother.

"Now can we finish, baby?" the woman asked interrupting his thoughts, her words slurred, whining, irritating.

"We're done." He tried to whisper.

She was slumped face down on *his* side of the bed, and red and black smears of makeup soiled *his* pillow. When she rolled over toward him, enormous ashen breasts, with nipples like fried eggs, flopped to each side of her colossal girth. "But you didn't do me no good,

26

sweetie, and you promised." She'd kept him up most of the night with her constant demands.

"Get your smelly ass up and go home," he groaned. The sound of his own voice forced his eyes shut. "No one could do you any damn good." He fumbled on the nightstand for his wallet, pulled out the last of what started out as two hundred dollars, and threw the money at her.

She stared at the bills. "Twelve measly bullshit dollars . . . I ain't no whore, and I damn shore ain't your mommy like you been callin' me all night, neither."

"Get your cunt out of my bed and go home, before I shoot your white ass," he said. "I only have a couple of hours to make a meeting." While waiting for her to move, but thinking of Juan Hernandez, he slid his 45 from under the pillow and released the magazine to check the load. When he met with the Mexican again, he would be prepared and would do things his way.

As his feet touched the floor, he again realized why he should never have mixed alcohol and drugs, even if the drug was as benign as cocaine. However, the sudden appearance of the Mexican had unnerved him to the point of needing a stiff drink. Just one, he'd thought, and maybe a line of coke, nothing serious, just enough to calm him down so he could think. Moreover, before he'd met the oversized woman and squandered his money and time on her, he'd concluded that there could be only one reason why the Mexican had given him another day to return the money: Juan Hernandez had been alone and was running

Mose Duane

a bluff. The Mexican had no way of getting the money from Johnny Bishop's safe without him.

Black Berry slammed the magazine back into the handle of the pistol and smiled. The metallic "click" was unmistakable.

The big woman jumped up and moved swiftly to her clothing, stark-white blubber rolling. "Listen, sweetie, I didn't mean nothin'. You're a good guy and all, and if'n twelve bucks is all's you got, don't you fret about it at all. And if'n you want to call me mommy, why that's okay too." She was trying to expand enormous panties over equally enormous thighs. The sight aroused him, and he grinned. Why he favored heavy women was beyond him, but there it was, and he lived with it. He aimed the pistol at a massive breast and held it there as she dressed.

"Listen, sweetie," she said as she hastily pulled on an odd assortment of clothing, "if'n I could just get me some of that candy from you before I leave, it would shore help. I mean when you judge all I done for you and all. Just a line or two, that's all."

"You're damn gutsy, aren't you? Considering you have a loaded pistol pointed at your titties." He grinned and realized that with her clothes on, even with smeared makeup, she was a fine-looking woman, and he understood why he'd picked her up at the bar and brought her home. The urge to shoot her had subsided along with the pounding in his head. He picked up a small white packet and tossed it to her.

"And the twelve dollars," she pointed to the money still on the bed, "can I keep that too? I mean my kids will need breakfast and all."

"When I get out of the shower, you'd better be gone," he said, "and make sure you use the money to feed your fat-ass kids."

He felt much better after he showered. The big woman was gone, and his hangover had diminished, to the point of leaving him with what he considered rational thoughts. He was down to less than an hour to meet with the Mexican, but that was more than enough time to go by the Velvet Rail and pick up the money first. He figured having the money with him would make it appear as though he were serious about returning it. He dressed in khaki slacks, a brown western shirt, his Stetson hat, and Tony Lama boots. All of which he'd bought to pamper himself. He hadn't dressed like a hillbilly from *Kentuckyana* since his first big win after leaving the hills of Bullitt County. Only the best for him, he'd decided long ago, and had grown to like it. He also pulled on a long silver studded, leather tasseled vest to conceal the ever-present pistol in his waistband. The vest also made him appear more Mexican than black, which he hoped would help mollify Juan, at least long enough for him to get off a clean shot or two.

Black Berry owned a silver replica 1957 Porsche Speedster convertible shell bolted onto a Volkswagen platform. He babied the car as if it was the real thing, and only those in the know could tell it from a genuine Speedster. He kept every chrome-plated nut, bolt, and gizmo polished bright, and didn't allow even a drop of oil to seep or spot the undercarriage. Even the metal flake, silver paint job was over the top compared to the car's actual worth, but he was willing to pay the extra for what he wanted. The Porsche even seemed to run better than usual as he drove toward the pool hall, and he was especially pleased with himself for having had the self-control not to blow any of his hard-earned cash on a new Mustang or Camaro or something equally impressive.

Not that the Volkswagen/Porsche Speedster wasn't impressive. It was in almost mint condition, including the paint job that shimmered like an emerald. And today was going to be an excellent day after all, Black Berry thought, as he allowed the small engine to rev aggressively, but smoothly, while shifting through the gears. He would retrieve the money, hand it to Juan to distract him, and then cleanly plant a bullet in his fat heart before he could say, hey *hombre* or *caramba,* or whatever his Spanish expression of the day might be. One shot, he figured, and since he'd have the surprise advantage that shouldn't be a problem.

He had finally resigned himself to the fact that there was no way in hell he was going to give up any part of what had now ballooned to over sixty grand in cash. It was his money as far as he was concerned. He'd worked for it; he'd expended an enormous amount of time and energy for it, so why should he simply hand it over? It wasn't his fault that the rat from Guatemala was allowed back across the border.

He'd do in the Mexican and soon be on his way to Canada. He figured he could be across the border before they found the body.

He also had to worry about his pool cues. He had time and money invested in those as well, and figured they were simply too valuable to abandon. He would offer them to Johnny Bishop at fifty cents on the dollar for a quick sale. He was sure the old man would jump at such a bargain, and at a chance to be rid of him for good. That would add another seven or eight-grand to his Canadian fund. "Yes, today's going to be a fine day," he said aloud and smiled as he downshifted to slow the Speedster.

He pulled into the dirty and lifeless quarter-acre parking lot in front of the Velvet Rail. The bent and sagging chain link fence at the rear divided it from the equally dull lot of a neglected strip mall. Both lots had several parked or abandoned vehicles scattered about. He was to meet with Juan to hand over the money in the parking lot behind the mall.

Black Berry parked, scanned both lots for the Mexican's limousine. Though not in sight, he knew it was there, hidden somewhere in the shadows between the buildings, with Juan lurking inside, shifty eyed like a fat reptile waiting to spring its trap. But Black Berry would pounce first, and he could hardly contain his enthusiasm as he quickly walked to the pool hall and fleetingly thought it strange that J.C.'s Honda wasn't parked in front of the side door blocking the entrance as usual. He pushed the splintered door open. "J.C., you here?" he hollered as he walked in. "What the hell happened to the door?" Soda cans and food baskets were still strewn about and none of the pool tables had been brushed in preparation for the coming day's use. "You better get your sagging ass in gear. You only got thirty minutes to open."

When no one answered, he walked to the office and shoved the door open. "J.C., where the hell—" and he froze, rock solid still, mouth open, eyes open, brain closed. Understanding was locked in the fog of his head until a light breeze blew through the room and ruffled small shreds of money that were strewn on the floor—his money. "Fuck!" he screamed. His mind whirled and he walked in small circles, his hands to the side of his head as if trying to keep it from exploding. "Fuck, fuck, fuck." His trigger finger moved involuntarily, like squeezing off rounds, one after another. "I'll kill them. I'll kill every last fucking one of them." The thundering boom, boom, boom was back in his head with a vengeance.

Ten minutes later, Black Berry burst through the front door of Johnny Bishop's house, pistol waving. "Where's my goddamn money?" he screamed.

Johnny looked up from the pool table, cigarette bobbing, barely hanging from his lips.

"Someone blew the safe and took it all, every damn dollar!" Black Berry shrieked, his head throbbing.

"No shit!" Johnny looked surprised.

"Look, you old fuck." Black Berry shoved the pistol into Johnny's chest. "Tell me now or I'll blow your heart out." Sweat poured down his beet red face.

Johnny took a hard drag from his cigarette. "Calm down, I don't know nothing about nothing."

Black Berry turned the pistol toward the wide eyed, cotton-white stranger who was crouched beside the tall spectator's chair on the opposite side of the pool table. "What the hell do you have to do with this?"

Eddy stood and held up his shaking hands. "Nothing man, I'm just playing—"

Black Berry fired. The shot pierced the blue shirt just at Eddy's right shoulder, well away from his heart, took out the collarbone, and shattered the window behind him. He swayed backward then lurched forward onto the pool table, and then rolled to the wooden floor with a thud.

"Someone had better start talking or you're both fucking dead." Black Berry screamed and hurried around the pool table. He placed the barrel of his 45 on the bleeding man's chest. "You pass out on me, you miserable bastard, you'll never wake up."

Scarcely holding consciousness, blood soaking his blue, sweat drenched shirt, Eddy managed to say, "Big man and a boy were here earlier . . . said they blew the safe and were going to Bayfield . . . and that Stony somebody had your cues and—"

Black Berry knew who the big man and boy were, and the only thing he heard after that was Bayfield. "Where the hell is Bayfield?"

"D-don't know."

Black Berry pulled the trigger.

The round punched a hole dead through Eddy's heart and on through the wood floor, drafting blood along with it. "I knew that goddamn wop had my money," he said and then turned to Johnny, but Johnny was running down the street as hard as his skinny old legs could carry him.

Five

In a rundown area of Redondo Beach, a row of individual three-room houses, painted rusty orange and named Sunset Shadows Manor, was home to numerous illegal south-of-the-border day laborers. J.C., Blondie when she wasn't running off to "God knows where," and Kid also called one of the undersized houses home and had for more than five years.

During the first few years of Kid's life, they'd lived in an upscale apartment in the Westwood area. That was back when J.C. could hold his own on any pool table in the state, or country for that matter. That was before he lost his ability or nerve or whatever, and long before he discovered sour mash and of course Black Berry, both a major downfall in his life. It perturbed him deeply that both these peculiarities of fate were from the great state of Kentucky. The home of beautiful women, fast racehorses, smooth bourbon, and now one mean son of a bitch who was out to do him in.

J.C. slowly pulled the Civic to the curb and made a quick check around. Black Berry's Porsche wasn't present. He parked, pulled the semiautomatic .22 caliber pistol from the glove box, motioned for Kid to follow, and hurried into the puny house.

Inside the house, he chambered a round into the lightweight pistol, handed it to Kid, and stationed him beside the bedroom door so he would be behind it if it opened. "If Black Berry comes in the door, he's here to

35

do us harm. You wouldn't spoil my day none if you shot him."

Kid's eyes opened as big and clear as thousand-dollar marbles.

J.C. thought about the boy for a moment. Why hadn't she taken him with her? Why did she leave the kid behind for him to look after? He could move much faster without dragging a kid along. Then again, that was her excuse for leaving him in the first place. *He would slow Rabbit and me down anyway*, she'd said in her note. Still, he figured she should have taken him. The boy was her responsibility.

"Look, just stand there and point," J.C. said, "but if you feel the urge pull the trigger, don't hesitate."

From under the unmade bed, he pulled out an old Samsonite suitcase, an even older pool cue case, and set both on the rumpled bedcovers. He opened the cue case and slid his Rambow out to make sure it was there. Of course, he knew it would be there, Blondie simply would not have taken the cue without the case, but he checked anyway. He placed the cue on the bed, and then quickly began packing the suitcase with clothes that might fit him or Kid; rags neither had worn in months, if not years, nothing more valuable than a dollar or two. All crap, he thought, that given the circumstances should plainly have been abandoned. Old habits, however, are hard to break. If you're leaving you pack a suitcase, it's ingrained. And no way was he going anywhere without his Rambow. What would he do for a living without his pool cue?

He was also thinking of taking the time to change his soot-soiled clothing when he heard a car door slam shut. He stood up straight and waited.

The bedroom door opened slowly, and then Black Berry stepped in. "Going someplace?" he asked in a controlled, calm voice. He held his 45 at his side.

"Taking a little trip up north," J.C. said, "to see Blondie's parents."

"You taking my money with you?"

"Don't know nothing about your money. Maybe you should go talk to Johnny."

"Done talked to him. He told me everything before I put a hole through his miserable heart."

Kid stepped sideways from behind the door. He held the small pocket pistol in both hands, pointed up at Black Berry. "You shot Johnny?" he asked, and tears rolled down his cheeks.

Black Berry turned to the boy. "Maybe not, maybe I was just kidding, maybe the old bastard got away."

"You ain't kidding. You're a bad man. Even mom said so." Kid's voice trembled. His hands shook and the pistol bobbed.

"That skinny bitch wouldn't know the difference between a good guy and a bad one," Black Berry said.

Kid raised his pistol higher, looking like he might fire.

Black Berry made eye contact. "Now you wouldn't shoot your old buddy Levi with that toy gun you got there for just kidding, would you?" He tapped his 45 on his thigh, his finger tightening around the trigger. "And did

37

you even cock the damn thing; you know it has to be cocked—"

He'd barely gotten the words out of his mouth when J.C. clubbed him across the side of the head with the butt of the Rambow, which produced a loud sickening "plop." Black Berry's eyes rolled up and he went slack and down. J.C. looked at the cue. It was still in one piece, so he hauled it over his head for another whack but couldn't do it. Not with the boy watching, he told himself.

He quickly returned the cue to its case, retrieved the pistol from Kid's trembling hands, and jammed it into his pocket. He then hurriedly checked the fridge. Eatables he ignored, but not the bottle of Wild Turkey 80. Along with the luggage and cue case, he carried the bottle out to the Honda and placed everything in the trunk beside the overstuffed backpack. The Joker's puffy expression hadn't changed. "Come on, kiddo," he said. "Since I'm stuck with you, let's go live like human beings for a change."

Six

In early 1960, along the rim of the Mogollon Plateau in north central Arizona, a diesel-powered Caterpillar shaved a swath of land of tall ponderosa and short piñon pines. The naked earth was then paved over to form a small private airstrip with a narrow parallel taxiway several yards to the south.

Twenty or so medium size cabins and an equal number of empty lots now ring the runway, most with direct access for a gaggle of small aircraft. The runway, one end marked 27 and the other 9, hugged the lay of the land with both ends twenty feet lower than the middle, and the airport had no control tower. All takeoffs and landings were blind free-for-alls.

Troy Forkner, J.C. Forkner's younger brother and acting police chief of Upland, Arizona, leaned back in a once white wooden lounge chair in the thick rye grass that divided the runway from the taxiway. He wore only denim jeans and flip-flops allowing the setting sun full view of his already cherry red shoulders. Holly Garcia, a long, bronzed legged, sun-browned brunette, stretched out on a blanket at his right absorbing the sunrays with no ill effects, was wearing possibly the skimpiest bikini legally allowed in Arizona.

They faced perpendicular to the direction of the runway to provide Troy the best view of both ends. He watched as two small single engine airplanes, one flying in from the south, the other from the north, entered the landing pattern at the same time. One landed on runway 27 and the other on 9, miraculously not trading propellers or pilots as they converged at the middle. Troy raised his bottle of Budweiser in salute to a job well done, even if by pure divine intervention. "Any landing you walk away from is a good one," he yelled at the pilots as if they could hear him.

On his left was a cooler of replenishments, all bottles—bottles being the only way to drink beer as far as he was concerned—and a neat row of dead soldiers surrounded the cooler. Also present were several flight manuals, his supposed reading for the day. Five months earlier, someone had taken notice of his canary yellow Waco biplane, with desert landscape emblazoned on both sides of the fuselage, performing barrel rolls over the town of Strawberry, and reported it to the Federal Aviation Administration and the Department of Public Safety. The FAA saw it as illegal aerobatics over a populated area and pulled his license for six months. To redeem himself with the agency, he had to pass a written exam and a flight check ride with an instructor less qualified than him.

Also because of the infraction, the town of Upland officially downgraded him from acting police chief to the boring job of cruising the streets of the small town as an regular patrolman for an undetermined amount of time.

Unofficially, however, because Upland had no one else qualified to take his place, he was now acting as the acting police chief.

He tossed another manual aside, it hit the stack with a surprising smack, and Holly jumped. "This is silly," he said. "I know all this crap."

"Calm down, you only have thirty days to go." Holly's voice sounded both soothing and encouraging as usual.

Troy smiled and settled back into his chair, thinking of Holly. She had come from Butte, Montana in the back seat of a Ford F-250 dragging a two-horse horse trailer courtesy of a rodeo star named Tex Bowman, headed for the *Region's Rowdiest Rodeo* in Upland, almost a year earlier. "If Tex could've ridden me as he did his horses we would never have parted," she'd told Troy the last week of the rodeo. That night, Troy had taken the challenge, and the girl. He now wondered if he'd done the right thing.

Troy could hear two more airplanes droning over the tall pines. He twisted the cap off another bottle of Budweiser, hoisted it to the clear blue sky. "Quiet on the set," he said as if directing a movie, "and action." The planes flew over the center of the airport, again one from the north and one from the south. This time both turned downwind and toward the same end of the runway, one extending its flight to allow the other to land first. "Much better," he called out and again raised his beer in a salute.

He then turned his attention back to the divine sculpture stretched out beside him and felt amazed that she did not stir him at all at that moment. Too much beer, or too much of a good thing, he told himself, or was he simply getting bored?

"Thirty days is all," she repeated.

"That's to get my pilot's license reinstated, but after that I just don't know . . . I could be done with this lawman shit because of the politics. Can you believe those assholes in town had the gall to demote me?"

Holly removed her sunglasses, rolled over on her stomach. If he didn't know she was wearing anything, he'd swear she wasn't. "Bureaucrats," she said, "even in a small town, are still bureaucrats. You're not going to quit, though. You don't know anything else."

"I could do lots of things. Fly for America West Airlines or one of the other big boys, maybe."

"And leave Upland? I don't think so."

"Yeah, I suppose you're right. So maybe I could join the rodeo circuit and ride with Cowboy Bob."

"Tex? Yeah, right. Now you are joking."

"Okay, so I don't know how to ride a frigging horse. I could learn, however. It can't be hard."

Holly looked at him with a wicked smile, her dazzling brown eyes glimmering in the sunlight. "You're right, it's easy. Come on inside and I'll teach you."

"You can't be serious," he said. "Don't you ever get tired?"

"Come on," she cooed, "you said you'd keep me happy."

"Drink a beer." He held one up, offering it to her.

"Will you help me work off the calories?"

Troy rolled his eyes.

But thirty minutes later, in the cabin on the northwest side of the runway, he was naked on the bed staring out of the uncovered picture window waiting for a glimpse of an airplane—any airplane—to slide by, gear down, flaps down, engine at idle on a glide path to a landing. Static filled mood music he didn't know wafted softly from the radio.

Holly, sun browned hair flailing, straddled him, pumping in long strokes, riding as hard as Tex Bowman rode his horses, the thought no doubt driving her to extremes. "This is how it's done, Troy, you dig your heels in and hold on," she said, and she dug her heels in and lurched up and down. Her nails dug into his chest, and she let out high-pitched squeals and drenched in sweat she finally collapsed flat onto him, gasping. Troy's thoughts, however, were on the wings of aircraft, floating slowly to earth, touching down with a gentle nudge of a grass-slicked runway.

Holly regained her strength, put her hands on his chest and shoved away. "You horse turd, you," she said. "We haven't known each other long enough for you to be passing out stiff dicks and calling it passion. You know that?"

"You got what you wanted, what the hell are you screaming about?"

"Look, you dumb shit." She now stood beside the bed butt naked, strings of hair stuck to her face, beads of sweat pooling between dynamic breasts. "When we make love, I want you thinking of me; not gazing out the window dreaming about some frigging . . . whatever."

"What? Are you now saying I'm a lousy lover? Are you going back to Cowboy Bob? Hell, I send you over the edge without even trying."

"Shit, Troy. You can't expect that pecker of yours to do it all."

Still on the bed, Troy placed his hands behind his head showing sculpted muscles, broad shoulders, a thin waist, and a still long, hard dick. "Why not?" He smiled proudly.

"Because there's more to it than just that, women want to be loved, pampered, treated special. They can get off with a frigging dildo. Is that all you want to be, a frigging dildo?"

"Every man's dream, darlin'—" he stopped, smiled "—hell every woman's dream."

She put her hands on her hips, flat belly heaving, deep brown eyes piercing.

He rolled his eyes downward and smiled again.

"Damn it, Troy. That's all you are, a frigging dildo. You'll never be a husband or father."

"Whoa, whoa, girl, nobody said anything about getting hitched or having kids. Where in the hell did that come from?"

Holly grabbed her jeans and pulled them on over her bare bottom.

From day one, Troy had appreciated the fact that she didn't wear panties or bra. "Tell you what, baby doll," he said. "Let's try it again. I'll do a better job this time. This time we'll make love."

"Kiss my ass."

"We can start there."

She went to the kitchen, retrieved a beer, and heaved it at him. Troy caught the bottle before it hit the headboard, or his head.

"Make love to that, you . . . you . . . you asshole. It seems to be the only thing you're capable of loving." She stormed out the door dragging her shirt behind her.

He twisted the cap off the bottle and allowed a quarter of the spewing brew to flow into his mouth and down his throat. He turned, looked out the window, and watched Holly pull her shirt on as she walked away from the cabin. "Shit," he said and frowned, "Maybe I love her. Maybe that's my problem."

An hour later, nude and shivering, Holly crawled back in bed beside Troy. She snuggled tight against him.

"Where'd you go?" he said and put his arm around her. He was more asleep than awake.

"For a walk, I wanted to think about things."

"Things?" he asked in a light and soft breathing voice.

"You know . . . me and you."

"What about me and you?"

"I love you," she said.

"Uh huh," he said.

"I think I'm pregnant."

"Uh huh," he said again, and his soft breathing turned to snoring.

Seven

When Black Berry came to, his head lay canted on the floor in a spatter of thick blood. He could make out lines of faint, blurry light that tunneled under the bed from the bathroom. His skull felt like a pulsating volcano ready to erupt. He tried to focus and arrange the pieces of the distorted puzzle of where he was and why he was there. Vaguely, he remembered the boy—J.C.'s boy—pointing the sissy pistol at his head and figured the kid must have pulled the trigger, and when he realized he could see from only one eye, he decided the shot must have taken the other. After several minutes, he forced himself off the floor and into the bathroom to assess the damage and disfigurement to a once perfect face. A hen's egg size knot protruded from his left temple and his left eye had swollen shut, but it was still there. He'd been blindsided, walloped upside the head with something solid and not shot, he concluded. "I'll pull that son of a bitch's nuts out for this while he's alive." He spoke to the now imperfect face in the mirror.

He fumbled through the medicine cabinet and found a bottle of pain pills, swallowed four or five, and shoved the bottle into a pocket. His desire for a payback exceeded his desire to simply sleep until the pain dissipated, so he forced himself out of the house and into his Porsche. He threw the 45 on the passenger's seat, within easy reach. "I'll kill that son of a bitch if it's the last thing I do," he mumbled as he started the car.

47

He'd been unconscious for a couple of hours, the sun had slid behind some of the larger buildings but, painfully, glared into his eye as it flashed between buildings. He took extra care in checking each side road and the rearview mirror for a long, black limousine. Juan Hernandez would be looking for him for sure.

With the thought of now needing money to chase down J.C., he drove back to the Velvet Rail. The parking lot and building seemed as dark and deserted as a midnight cemetery, though a trickle of lost souls milled around the front door. With J.C. on the run, no one had shown up to open the doors or turn on the lights for business. Black Berry parked the Porsche at the back of the building and quietly entered through the damaged side door. Inside, he stopped and listened, and could hear only the sound of the compressors of various coolers and refrigerators. Carefully he picked his way through the dark poolroom, around the snack bar counter, and into the office. Again, he stopped and listened, and again could hear only the hum of equipment. He switched on a light and waited for his eye to adjust to the blast of overhead florescent brightness from the only fixture still intact. When his eye finally focused, he saw nothing had been touched: the safe in pieces and the shredded and scattered scraps of what was left of his money were as he'd left them. Quickly, he dropped to his knees, began collecting tens and fives, and charred but recognizable, pieces of others.

"Hey, *gringo*, what the hell has happened?"

Black Berry recognized the baritone voice of Juan Hernandez but did not look up. "We were robbed," he answered, and simultaneously fumbled at his back for his 45. When he realized he'd left the pistol on the seat of the Porsche, he repeated himself, "We've been robbed."

"You may have been robbed, *hombre*, but I do not get robbed."

"It was *your* money they took!"

"You no *comprende* the English, huh?" Juan asked. "It is in your safe, it is your *dinero*. It is in my safe, it is my *dinero*."

"I know who took it," Black Berry said as he finally looked up. Juan stood inside and left of the doorway. He was a short, stout man with a seemingly pleasant smile and slicked back black hair. He wore his usual casual but expensive business suit. Standing in the doorway behind Juan, wearing an outlandish black derby hat with a pink band, black suit with salmon shirt, pink tie, and pink handkerchief that fluffed from his breast pocket, stood a linebacker of a man. His hands, folded in front of him church style, held an S&M .45 caliber X-tream pistol with a silenced and chromed Lothar barrel. Black Berry had never seen an X-tream, but knew instantly what it was, and felt a trickle of wetness run down his leg when he realized what would have happened had he not left his own pistol in the car. Droplets of sweat trickled into his eye. He wanted to wipe it but dared not move.

"*Caramba!*" Juan said and smiled a toothy grin when he saw Black Berry's face. "They clobber you *mucho* plenty."

"I'm not shitting you, Juan, I know who took your money and if you give me more time, I'll bring it back along with the guy's nuts . . . on a platter."

"If I want *testículos*, I take yours. What I want is my *dinero*."

"If you let me walk, I swear you'll get it—every dollar."

"Plus the interest." Juan gestured at the man behind him. "My brother, José, and me . . . we do not work *por gratis*."

"Plus interest," Black Berry agreed. "But look, could you spot me a hundred or so? I mean, I'll need some cash to get to them, to get your money back."

"José!" Juan spoke loudly and snapped his fingers. "Shoot this *gringo* for being *estúpido*. I am tired of messing with him."

In two steps, the big man had his massive S&M pistol pointing at Black Berry's head.

"No. No. Wait." Black Berry cowered toward the floor and covered his head with his hands. "I have more than ten grand worth of pool cues in the back room. You can use them for collateral."

"*Hombre*—" Juan smiled again and held up his hand for José to stop "—you got no cues. We look already. No cues."

"Jesus, shit," Black Berry said and suddenly remembered what the pool player had tried to tell him. "Okay, okay. I think I know where my cues are too. And I can probably stick enough of these bills together—" he held out a fistful of burnt bills "—to find the guy who took your money. Just let me go look for him. What do you have to lose?"

Juan Hernandez smiled at Black Berry and the scorched dollars. "Three days, *amigo*, after that José will come to talk with you. He had to go to *México* to finish the job you started but did not complete. That squealing son of a pig from Guatemala wasn't even frightened enough to shut up, so the *dinero* is now José's, and I think he wants it." Juan turned and walked out of the room.

José held up three fingers, smiled, his large mouth stretching ear to ear, and then he too turned and left the room.

Black Berry waited kneeling on the floor until it was quiet, until he was confident that the Hernandez brothers were gone. "Brothers, my ass," he muttered as he got up and franticly began tearing through the office. "They must be goddamn twins." He upended file cabinets, desktops, and operational desk drawers. Those mangled beyond functioning, he grabbed by their handles and whirled them into the wall in a fit of anger. Finding anything that might contain some record of where J.C. and family would have gone in Bayfield appeared hopeless.

About to give in to the possibility of driving around the unfamiliar town of Bayfield, *wherever the hell that is*, until he found J.C.'s old Honda, he suddenly remembered the wall of records. Low voltage portrait lights faintly illuminated the wall. He quickly found Blondie's picture, and next to it was a short article about her win in Vegas, including her name being Straub before she became a

Forkner, and her hometown of Bayfield, California was two hundred miles northeast of L.A.

When José Hernandez left the Velvet Rail he drove the limo down the street, made a U-turn and parked with the building in view. Juan, however, had stayed in the shadows in the poolroom and watched Black Berry as he studied the pictures on the wall and then rushed from the building. Before Juan left, he also scanned the pictures and read the article about the pool playing beauty from Bayfield, California.

Eight

"**Can** I help you?" the big man known as Stony asked as he stepped from the back room when Black Berry walked into Stone's Pawn Shop. Stony wore baggy camouflage trousers and vest with no shirt. Middle aged, bulky, but defined, with a receding hairline, he looked like the kind of single man who worked out on a regular basis fighting the slow and startling pull of gravity and time, but still thought of himself as appealing to women. He was the kind of man that captured Black Berry's feral attention.

"Glad you're still open," Black Berry said.

"When I'm working late, I stay open." A smile flashed quickly then disappeared.

"Do you know who I am?" Black Berry asked.

Wide eyed, Stony stared at Black Berry's battered face. "Can't say as I do."

"I stopped in to see if you have any pool cues," Black Berry glanced around; the shop was long and narrow with floor to ceiling shelves overflowing with tools, small appliances, electronics, and other well used or worn-out items. Waist high glass cases lined both sides and one end of the room. An old National cash register dominated the case at the end. Displayed beneath the register he recognized half a dozen of his most expensive cues. Behind that case, a three-quarter wall with a closed door hid the backroom.

"Pool cues?" Stony questioned, again flashing a quickly disappearing smile, before his mouth tightened. "You're the guy from the pool hall, the guy who sells pool cues for Johnny Bishop. Are you looking for some to resell, I got some nice ones over here—" he pointed a nervous finger toward the display of cues "—these came from Vegas a couple of days ago."

"Well, son of a bitch, Vegas, huh?" Black Berry said. "How much for that one?" he pointed to one of his prized Balabushkas.

"Fifteen hundred."

"Too much . . . got anything cheaper?"

"Nope, this is all I have."

"Are you sure?"

Stony ignored the question. "What the hell happened to your face?" His quick and gone smile was now nervous.

"Had a fight with someone who tried to screw with me," Black Berry said and laid a stack of seared and torn fives and tens on the glass top. "I got a couple hundred."

Stony greedily looked at the money for a second. "Like I said, this is it and they came from Vegas a couple of days ago."

"Let's take a look." Black Berry opened the short gate between the low display cases that led to the backroom door.

"Hey, man, you can't go in there."

Black Berry pulled his pistol, "Sure I can," he gave Stony a shove with the barrel.

The backroom was half the size as the front. Appliances in various stages of repair filled wooden workbenches along the walls. Another workbench, covered with pool cues—his cues—still in their original plastic wrappers, occupied the middle of the room. A small stack of cardboard boxes already packed with cues were on the floor beneath the workbench, awaiting shipment. Several other cues were still joined and leaning against the workbench.

"They all came from Vegas," Stony quickly said, his eyes shifting, "and I can prove it."

"That's no fucking way to treat pool cues!" Black Berry yelled. "You can't lean them like that." He shoved his pistol in his waistband and began picking up the leaning cues and laying them flat on top of the workbench.

Stony watched and said nothing.

"You knew they were mine when you bought them!" Black Berry continued to yell. "That's the same as stealing from me!"

"Look. Okay. I didn't actually buy them in Vegas myself. A couple brought them in . . . they said *they* bought them in Vegas and that *they* owned them."

"You bought them from that fat ass wop J.C., and you knew they weren't his."

"I bought them from his wife and some damn hippie. They told me the cues were from Vegas, I swear." Stony closed the distance between him and Black Berry. "Tell you what, though, they're all here, and if you really

55

think they're yours, you can buy them back. I paid three grand for them."

Black Berry picked up another cue and sighted down it to see if it was still straight before laying it on the flat workbench. He looked at Stony and grinned. "No, I got a better idea," he said in a calmer voice. "I need money and planned on selling them anyway, so you give me six grand cash and I'll walk away. They're worth twice that, and you know it."

"Screw you, you little wetback. I don't have to do anything for you. You go bring the cops with a search warrant and try to prove they're yours. I have a receipt and a sworn statement of ownership."

Black Berry continued walking around the workbench placing cues on it. "You know what you can do with your bullshit receipts and statements don't you? I thought you said you knew who I was?"

"I'm not scared of you, you little worm, if that's what you think." Stony followed him around the workbench. "It's your only choice, you miserable turd bucket. Now get the hell out of here before I put my fist to the other side of your face." His absurd smile had turned into an absurd scowl.

Black Berry pulled his 45, but before he could level it, Stony nailed him with a massive, solid fist, on the opposite side of the head that J.C. had damaged. He flew backward, hit the floor hard," but managed to hold onto the pistol. Stony grabbed a hammer from a workbench and swung it. Black Berry rolled sideways as the hammer whizzed past his head and slammed onto the floor. He rolled completely over, brought the pistol up and fired.

The shot caught Stony in the abdomen; he went down in shock and agony. Black Berry jumped up and shoved the pistol into Stony's chest. "It's not my only choice, *turd bucket,* whatever the hell that means," he said and pulled the trigger. The shot blasted through Stony's heart, hit the concrete floor, ricocheted sideways, and tore a hole out the side of his chest. Blood spewed into a substantial puddle.

"You idiot," Black Berry said, "you could have survived this. All I wanted was money." He knelt beside the body and quickly found keys and a wallet. The wallet contained sixteen dollars. Black Berry frowned as he tenderly fingered Stony's bicep and forearm then moved down to his inner thigh and slowly up to his crotch and patted there. "What a waste," he said. "What a damn waste."

He hurried to the front of the store, opened the cash register, and found only forty-two dollars. "Hey turd bucket," he hollered over his shoulder, "how can you run a business with no goddamn money?" He shoved the few bills into his pocket and slowly wandered around the shop looking for a safe or something of real value but found only junk.

On a piece of white paper, using a black felt pen, he printed: CLOSED FOR VACATION, taped it to the front window, and locked the front door. He walked behind the gun cabinet and pocketed two boxes of .45 caliber cartridges, then pulled his Balabushka from the glass case.

"I guess you bought the rest for fifty-eight bucks, turd bucket," he told the very dead Stony as he left through the back entrance, also making sure to lock that door.

Nine

The next morning, Troy and Holly were up early packing the airplane with the few belongings they had brought to the cabin. The only things left in the refrigerator were a couple bottles of Budweiser.

"I'm hungry," Holly complained.

"It's only a forty-five-minute flight to Upland; we'll get breakfast at the airport."

Developed to accommodate rodeo fans from across the nation, Upland's airport was large for a town of its size. Cross-country and local pilots also knew it as a great stopover for fuel and comfort food.

"Not the way you fly. You always take the long way."

"It is after all a sightseeing adventure. It won't be boring."

Their exchange was light meaningless banter, stating the obvious and avoiding eye contact, neither mentioning the night before.

"What happens if you get caught flying with a suspended license?"

"The only way that's going to happen is if we crash and burn, and then it won't matter."

"That's a happy thought." Holly had not been in a small airplane until she'd met Troy and had described her first flight as five minutes of sheer horror, an hour of monotony, and five more minutes of sheer horror. Now though, after several trips, her feelings toward it had changed. She still got nervous on takeoffs and landings, but flights over the snow-covered San Francisco Peaks of Flagstaff, over the vastness of the Grand Canyon, over the rugged wonderment of Hoover Dam could only be described as spectacular. In addition, the weekly flights along the Mogollon Rim, over Payson, and over the red rocks of Sedona between Troy's cabin at the airpark and the Upland airport were nothing short of magnificent. To make it even more pleasant, Troy never did anything wild while she was onboard, no maneuvers outside those necessary for a smooth and safe flight.

The flight back to Upland was no different, smooth, and beautiful. The aircraft had open tandem cockpits, with Holly sitting in the front and Troy in the rear. Both wore communication headsets that also muffled the roar of the radial engine and blasting wind.

"One day I'm going to make the trip solo," Holly said, enjoying a sight reserved only for birds and those few who had taken the time to become private pilots.

"I'd bet on it," Troy answered. After a sweeping U-turn put the town of Jerome off the right wing to give Holly an up-close view, he retarded the throttle and pulled the nose of the Waco up slightly to put it into slow flight at the same altitude of a mining town that was built into the mountainside with the backsides of most houses precariously supported by tall slender stilts. "So, you're pregnant?" he asked as the plane settled and the roar abated.

"What's the huge brick building?" she asked as if she hadn't heard him. "It looks out of place."

"It was a hospital. Back in its boom days when the mines were going full bore, I guess Jerome thought it was going to be a metropolis. The monstrous abandoned thing at the top of that knoll is the Grand Hotel, and the structure directly off our right wing is the old high school complex."

"Oh," she said as if she understood any of it and took in as much as she could of the quickly passing town while mulling over her situation. A situation in which she had put herself despite taking what she thought were adequate precautions, precautions that were extremely important to her. She'd been born in a small town in Montana where her grandfather was the minister of the only church and had insisted on a marriage when Holly's mother became pregnant with her. Holly's father was a Mexican immigrant working for her grandfather as a ranchero on the family's ranch. Her mother's pregnancy was an embarrassment and inconvenience to the family, a thing to be dealt with before the baby was born. Though her parents had stayed married, they never really loved each other, and Holly had known that from a very young age. Her mother existed in isolation and forced shame, and Holly had no intentions of ever living that way. She would consider an abortion before she followed her mother's path.

Finally, after a long silence, she said, "It's yours, you know."

"What?"

"The baby, it's yours."

"I never doubted it, so what's the game plan?"

61

"Haven't given it much thought."

"I thought that's what you did last night, during your walk?"

"The rodeo is next week, and I'd really like to concentrate on that for now."

"No doubt," he answered.

The rest of the flight was uneventful and without conversation until Troy was cleared for landing.

"Wah-co 73 Romeo, you're number three." It was the morning shift controller, Beth McDonald.

As usual, Troy's landing was pure silk.

Ten

The nation's largest oil spill on record, a gusher in 1910, gave rise to the town of Bayfield, California. The oil spewed from a wooden derrick for almost eighteen months. Over a million barrels covered the sandy soil and turned it into gooey asphalt. The smell of oil and money beguiled a multitude of roughnecks and oil executives alike. They showed up in droves, and the oil pumps had been running—and leaking—nonstop since. The stench of oil permeated the earth, the air, the buildings, and Black Berry assumed the people of the oil slick town.

The drive up from L.A. had taken six hours instead of the three or four he'd figured on. He'd stayed on the freeways and never exceeded the speed limit, to avoid the law for sure, but more to protect his prized Speedster from the strain and possible damage of California's excessively rough, politically ignored, and hilly back roads. The four-cylinder Volkswagen engine complained and labored up the hills out of Santa Clarita, something he hadn't anticipated and something that would absolutely have to be taken care of as soon as he got his money back. Then, a massive tractor-trailer had reduced a compact car to a pile of blood-covered scrap outside of Lebec. It took two hours to clear a lane around the carnage, and there was no way to tell the make or model of the car. He wasted a good deal of time assuring himself that it wasn't J.C.'s Honda, with *his* money onboard.

He planned on stopping at a pay phone, scanning the phonebook to locate any Straubs listed, and then driving past each address in hopes of finding J.C.'s car. If that failed, he figured he'd call each number listed until he found someone who knew someone who knew Blondie or her family. How many Straubs could there possibly be in such a small town, he reasoned, especially if all of them are related and everyone knew everyone, like all the Berry brothers, sisters, uncles, aunts, and cousins in his home county south of the Ohio River?

However, unlike L.A., by nightfall, Bayfield shuttered its doors and windows and emptied its streets, looking as vacant and eerie as a moonlit ghost town, as if sundown would bring forth ghouls or demons of the past to be avoided at all costs. Black Berry made two passes along an empty and dreary Main Street, what he assumed was downtown, and found to his frustration but not surprise, not one public phone booth.

The thought of spending the night in the stench and gloom of "Oilsville" irritated him, but seeing no way out, he pulled into a parking lot of a building that had been a Dairy Queen sometime in its past. The structure had recently been painted in blue and white checks and converted to a local joint called Dick's Burgers, which of course was closed for the night. Black Berry pulled to the back of the deserted parking lot where there were no lights and backed into a space beneath a small overhanging tree, away from possible morning foot traffic.

He cranked down the windows. The Speedster had no air-conditioning. Sleeping in the claustrophobic space did not appeal to him, but at that point he had no choice. He pulled out a small bag of marijuana, rolled a thin joint, fired it up, and pulled the sweet smoke deep into his lungs. On the radio, Buck Owens was claiming to have a tiger by the tail, a song Black Berry older brother aped often when they were kids because of its reference to cocaine. Black Berry never knew his father, but his brother, who injected himself into the father role whenever he wanted to be malicious, raised him. His mother was around back then, but only when she wanted to be, and usually only when it met her needs and desires.

He'd scraped up more than enough money for hotel, food, and fuel, assuming he found J.C. quickly. If, however, his search was prolonged, he could be destitute in a hurry. Better safe than sorry, he figured, as his powerful desire to find J.C. had reached heights greater than anything even he could have imagined, certainly greater than his need for at home comfort.

Had he brought along any kind of liquor, he would again be breaking his self-imposed code of no drinking while on a job. He had no such code for drugs however, especially marijuana, cocaine, or his personal choice LSD. He possessed a full sheet of the mind expanding— promised to be fabulously potent—drug neatly folded in his vest pocket. He stubbed out his smoke, placed the roach in his pocket for later, pulled out the sheet, unfolded it, tore off a tab, and laid that on his tongue. "Just enough to ease my throbbing headache and ease my mood," he told himself, "Just enough to make me blissfully unaware."

Meticulously, he refolded the sheet and stowed it back in his pocket for safekeeping. He positioned the 45 at arm's length on the floor then removed his vest, rolled it into a tight wad, and tucked it beneath his head. He curled up across the bucket seats, allowing his good eye to be somewhat exposed to whatever the ghostly town might conjure up during the night.

As the potent narcotic worked its wonders, his head soared, and he was no longer anchored to the bucket seats by gravity but floating within the confines of the undersized vehicle. Portals began to open in his veiled subconscious mind, taking him back to the warm memories of his childhood, snuggling close to his mother.

"Mommy," he murmured.

"No, no," she softly answered, "you mustn't call me mommy when we're in bed."

"Okay?"

"Put your hand here and rub."

Little Levi Berry placed his small hand on the side of her large breast and squeezed.

"Gently," she said. "And move down, all the way down."

He complied, and her voluminous body engulfed him. She then began fondling him. First caressing his face, then his chest, his stomach, and more, much more, and something magically wonderful happened.

Drifting in the vastness of the universe within the diminutive car, Black Berry became blissfully aware of his erection, and he snuggled close to the phantom of his past as his heart raced, as he anticipated what was to come.

"I love you, mommy," he said, and slowly drifted into a drug induced sleep.

Eleven

Of course, J.C. had never intended on driving to
Bayfield; he just needed insurance in case Johnny Bishop
folded under the rage of Black Berry. He knew Blondie
would not visit her parents before striking out with Rabbit
for the big time up in Chicago. Her parents had not yet
forgiven her for marrying a common pool hustler with no
prospects of ever becoming anything more than a beaten
down thug and would always blame him for taking her
away from them. It pained him now to think that they
were right. He'd once had great visions of being a famous
player in the way of Greenleaf, Caras, Hoppe, Mosconi,
Hurricane Higgins, or even Minnesota Fats. Instead, he'd
become that beaten down thug, a thief, a murderer—a
dead man himself for sure. Furthermore, the fact that he'd
dragged along a thirteen-year-old to meet the same fate
only showed what a sorry soul he had become. Of course,
he shouldn't take all the blame, he told himself. After all,
Blondie could have taken the boy with her. It would have
been the only way to guarantee his survival.

Instead of Bayfield, he and Kid drove east on
Interstate 10 to San Bernardino, left the freeway and
snaked through the mountains to Big Bear Lake. There
was no way Black Berry would follow them, not in that
glorified pretend Porsche of his, because he rarely left the
freeways and J.C. knew it.

In Big Bear City, they checked into a resort hotel.
The finest J.C. could find on such short notice. In the

68

hotel's four-star restaurant, they ate crab legs galore that were swimming in buttery sauce, piles of garlic mashed potatoes, sweet baby carrots, and carrot cake heaped with thick, rich icing.

The following morning, they had an unhurried breakfast of omelets and hot tea in the same elegant restaurant. Time meant nothing, they weren't deliberately slow, but were in no hurry either as they meandered around Big Bear City taking in sites that could not have been more different from L.A. if it had been planned. Father and son, together and unapologetically eating stone cold ice cream and extra thick, candy laden milkshakes, foot long hotdogs and deep-fried onion rings. They lived as if they had not a worry in the world.

"Isn't all this stuff fattening?" Kid said smiling and patting his swollen stomach as they finally headed back to the car.

"That's what money will do for you," J.C. answered. "That's what real money will do."

"Make you fat?"

"Buy you things, young man . . . whatever you want. We'll worry about getting fat tomorrow. Today let's just enjoy the buying power while we have it, and while we have the time."

"But isn't it really Black Berry's money, Pop?"

"No son. These are ill gotten funds, acquired by dishonest means."

"Okay, but that doesn't make it ours."

"From the sale of narcotics probably, or proceeds of a hired gun maybe, and it belongs to whoever has it.

When Black Berry's employers had it, it was theirs. When Black Berry had it, it was his. Now we got it."

"But we stole it."

"Stole, now that's harsh . . . I found it in a feeble tin box, of sorts, so I kept it. If the government finds it on us, they'll take it and keep it. Are they thieves? Well they are, but that's a different story. The point is it belongs to whoever is in possession of it. And today, that's us."

Two more hours of shopping and they still left Big Bear by high noon, the old Honda squeaking and squealing as they pushed cross-country on state highways and county roads paralleling Interstate 40 until they reached Needles, California where they cut north to Laughlin, Nevada.

J.C. remembered the first time he was in Laughlin, when he was very young, not much older than Kid is now. At that time, there was only the Riverside Casino sitting on the river with a helicopter moored on the roof. Though small, the casino seemed gigantic, but the helicopter had impressed him as much as the casino. Now, though, the Riverside was a monster resort hotel and casino, with a helicopter sitting on the roof, and that still impressed him.

J.C. slowly drove past the Riverside and along Casino Drive to view the flashy casinos that made up Laughlin: Colorado Bell, Aquarius, Harrah's, Edgewater, and on and on until they passed ten in total.

"Just like Las Vegas," Kid said.

"Hardly as big," J.C. told him. "But impressive none the less." He made a U-turn and started back down Casino Drive. "Where do you want to stay?"

"Anyplace, they're all cool."

J.C. couldn't resist, so they checked into the Riverside Resort and Casino. He had not been in any gambling casino in years, but the constant ding, ding, ding, ding of the slot machines made him feel as if he had never left this one.

"Are we going to gamble away the money?" Kid asked.

"Or we could double it. That's what I had in mind, craps, or blackjack maybe."

"I read that the casinos have all the odds," Kid said, "that we can't really win, you know, in the long run they take it all, and that everything in the building was bought and paid for by other people's money."

"Well hell, son. How old are you?" J.C. asked as he fished a cigarette out of a crumpled pack and popped it between his teeth. "I really thought this was going to be a good idea, and fun."

"Not really," Kid said. "I think we should hang onto what we have. Why would we want to take the chance of giving it away to these guys? They have enough."

"Okay, okay. What are you now, my banker? I knew I should have left you in California."

"You don't really mean that, do you?"

"Well, I have to admit, and this is the honest truth, son—" J.C. set the cigarette ablaze, took a drag and blew out a couple of smoke rings "—you are starting to grow on me."

Kid's grin stretched the limits of his small face. "In that case," he said, "maybe you should quit smoking too."

"Don't push your luck, kiddo, but as far as gambling goes, I'll hold off for a while. Let's go get something to eat, and maybe do a little more shopping, and a little sightseeing, and then maybe sleep on it, how's that for starters?"

"Fair enough," Kid said.

They had another huge, satisfying dinner in the hotel's dining room and called it a day.

Twelve

Black Berry was startled awake by the backfire of a motor scooter grinding to a stop beside his vehicle. A thin young blonde climbed off the scooter, removed her helmet allowing the rest of her golden locks to fall to her shoulders with a couple of sensual shakes of her head. She walked toward Dick's Burgers without noticing the Speedster or him inside it. Although the ever-present stink of oil permeated the air, he felt clearheaded and now wide awake, unfettered by the acid induced memory-jolting veracity of the night before.

He considered finding an appropriate breakfast restaurant—eggs over easy, bacon, grits, OJ, and coffee sounded good. Instead, still bent on saving money, he blew four bucks on a Dick's Burgers breakfast special: a greasy chopped burger with cheese and egg scrambled into it, and a coffee tasting as if it were dredged directly from one of the many oil wells in the area. The motor scooter girl had a table to herself. He smiled and she smiled back. He considered the virtues of a skinny girl but couldn't come up with anything he thought interesting or worthwhile, so finished the thick brew and left.

He drove to a service station, filled the tank, and found an oil-soaked phonebook. Three Straubs were listed, all with phone numbers and addresses. He blew another three bucks on a street map of Bayfield. He hadn't watched his spending that closely since leaving Kentucky, and he didn't like it. However, he was now

73

ready to complete his business and move on to better things.

Sticking to his original plan, he drove to the first address, which was located on the north side of town. The neighborhood consisted of old clapboard houses with wire fences and no sidewalks. J.C.'s beat up Honda wasn't around, so Black Berry followed First Street south and wandered through another neighborhood until he found the second address. That neighborhood seemed to be in better condition than the first, with brick houses and green lawns, but again no Honda. Then, ten blocks to the west, he found the third address. He parked and surveyed the house for a moment. Though there was no Honda, he felt positive this was the kind of place Blondie's parents would live in: Big—big property, big shade trees, big pool, and a big motor home parked in the side yard under the shade of a canvas awning. The house also looked like it would have room for a pool table, one a young woman could learn to play on.

He walked onto the expansive porch and rang the doorbell. When the door opened, the beauty of the woman standing before him surprised him. Her wrinkle free, round, double chinned face, beamed. Her girth expanded with oversize breasts and hips. Black Berry could imagine himself fondling the warm vastness of her rolling body.

"May I help you?" Her voice was high, sexy. Her breath smelled of grape wine.

Hi, my name is Billy," Black Berry said. "I'm looking for some friends of mine from L.A., J.C. and Blondie Forkner."

"Well, Blondie is my daughter, but . . . oh, my, young man, what happened to your face?"

Black Berry's eye was still swollen, but not shut. "I had a traffic accident a couple of days ago. Is Blondie here? I owe her some money, and I just happened to be passing by and figured I'd deliver it."

"I haven't seen her in months, but I'm sure she's in Los Angeles, at that pool hall, with that no-account pool shark . . . such a waste. She would have been much better off staying here and working for her father at the oil company, or marrying some local oil rigger, instead of running off with that worthless piece of humanity."

"Is her father home?"

"He's at work where he always is, daylight to dark . . . and if you find Blondie, you tell her, her father could use some help."

"I probably won't be back to L.A. for a while. Can I come in and give you her money?"

"Why, where are my manners? You come on in. Would you like a glass of wine? I just opened it this morning."

"That'd be great, Missus Straub. Are you alone?"

"I'm always alone and call me Phyllis. It's not the good stuff, Ralph won't buy me the good stuff anymore, says I drink too much of it."

The Thomasville and Broyhill feel, and smell of the house was not lost on Black Berry even as his attention was drawn to her waddle as they made their way to a kitchen full of Sub Zero stainless. Her enormous hips rippled up, down, and side to side even though she tried to hide them in a large baggy skirt.

In the kitchen, he politely took a seat at the round, glass topped table and watched as she poured wine from a gallon carton into a crystal tumbler and, with a broad smile, handed it to him. She then poured herself a drink, placed the carton on the table, and settled next to him, in what was obviously her chair because of the ample space around it.

"To you, Phyllis," Black Berry said and raised his glass to her.

She smiled, "thank you, and to you, umm."

"Billy," Black Berry repeated then sipped a healthy sampling of the wine. It was bitter and stronger than he'd expected.

"Billy," she echoed and emptied her glass with one long swallow then poured another. "And what were we discussing?"

"Your love life," Black Berry said and grinned.

"Now you know that's not a nice thing to say to a lady."

"A beautiful lady," he corrected her.

"I haven't been called that in years." She giggled lightly.

"Well, it's your husband's loss."

"I thought you came in here to give me Blondie's money."

Black Berry took another sip of the bitter liquid then downed the rest. "The truth of the matter is, I don't have any money. I just told you that to get you alone."

"What does that mean?"

"It means I find you very attractive and I'd like to take you to the bedroom and—"

"Why, Billy, what's going on here? Do you have a fetish for large women?"

"Absolutely, and right now you're on top of my list."

Phyllis put her glass to her lips and watched him for a moment, as if thinking about his proposal then said, "I think you should leave, before this gets out of hand."

Black Berry smiled, pulled out his 45 and placed it on the tabletop. "This is already out of hand and could be quite enjoyable if it doesn't get ugly."

Phyllis looked at the pistol then looked at his eyes. "Well, I sure as hell don't want it to get ugly." Her glazed teal eyes sparkled as she pushed herself from the table and wobbled down the hallway, toward the bedroom.

He picked up the pistol, tucked it into his waistband, poured himself another hefty tumbler of wine, and followed, watching. Up, down, left, right.

"Are you going to force me to commit adultery?" she asked as soon as they were in the bedroom, "to fornicate against my will?"

Black Berry laughed. "Adultery? Fornicate? Are you some kind of a religious nut?"

"Lord no. I'm just asking . . . are you going to force yourself on me?"

"No, I'm going to make love to a beautiful woman. Now, take all your clothes off."

"That's not very romantic."

"I don't have time for romance."

"Well, exactly what are you going to do?"

"First, I'm going to find your stash and I don't want you to go running off while I'm not watching you."

"Stash? You mean money? Is that what this is all about?"

"Why, Phyllis, you sound disappointed." He held his finger up as if it was a pistol and pressed it deep between her heaving breasts. "If you even look like you're going to scream or run, I'll have to put a hole right through your beautiful heart, and that would break mine. So, lovely lady, take your clothes off."

She glared at him, and her mouth puckered. "I thought you were going to be nice to me."

"I am being nice, but first things first. I can't have you running out of the house when I'm not looking. Surely you understand that?"

"You're not going to hurt me, are you?" she asked, and began to undress.

Black Berry backed away and watched, took a sip of his wine, but savored every second of the spectacle of her undressing. "Now, lie down on the bed," he said, "with those gorgeous tits pointing up."

"Promise you won't hurt me," she said with a muffled, but clear voice as she followed instructions.

Using her ample bra and panties, he tied her to the bedposts spread eagle, and stuffed a stocking in her mouth.

"Now, Phyllis, if you lie there like a good girl, we'll have a good time. Okay?"

She nodded yes.

Black Berry let out a sigh of relief as he slowly walked around the room removing his clothing. "This is nice," he said, pleased with the expensive surroundings. He ran his fingers over the fine furnishings. "I could get used to this," he continued as he walked to the bathroom. "Yes ma'am, very, very nice. Tell you what, if you promise to behave yourself, I'll take a quick shower."

She nodded affirmatively.

In the substantial, white tiled bathroom, he enjoyed a relaxing shower and carefully shaved his disfigured face. When he came out, clean and smelling like rosemary shampoo, Phyllis was fighting her bindings, but hadn't worked herself loose. He stood in front of her as naked as she was. "Are you trying to be a bad girl?"

She frantically nodded no.

"Well, maybe you should," he said and smiled. "After all you look great; maybe you could be a little bad for me." He downed the remainder of his wine, slid into bed beside her, and began fondling her enormous breasts. When he shook them, she shimmied and trundled like a creamy white rolling sea. He kissed one nipple then the other.

She let out a soft moan.

"That's wonderful, mommy," he said softly and caressed and kissed and licked each fold of her glorious body. Taking his time, he moved downward, past her capacious belly, kissing and fondling, and she flinched and moaned loudly.

Black Berry looked up at her and smiled. She was breathing heavily through her nose. "If I remove the stocking, will you behave?"

She fervently nodded yes.

He pulled the garment from her mouth, and she took a deep breath.

"God," she said, "don't stop now."

The wine was stronger than he'd expected. His head spun slightly as he closed his eyes and passionately kissed her. "I love you mommy," he softly muttered.

She returned the kiss, and in the next fifteen minutes, he took her on a bed-rattling joyride, one she surely had not experienced in years, if ever. She'd bucked, tossed, and whimpered, and then gave out a guttural, almost masculine, groan of satisfaction.

He remained on top of her for several more minutes, snuggling in the warm buoyancy of her voluminous body. "That was nice," he finally said as he rolled from her. "Now tell me where your stash is, and I'll go away and leave you alone."

"What if I don't want you to go?" She was still laboring for breath.

"I'll be back," he said and again looked over the posh furnishing in the bedroom and knew what he said was not a total lie. If things had worked out differently, he would surely move in here. "If at all possible, I'll be back, and you can count on it."

"You're crazy," she said.

"Now be nice, Phyllis. I thought we had a good thing going."

"We do," she agreed and smiled. "It was a compliment."

"In that case, I need money."

"What makes you think I have any?"

"Come on, all you rich babes have money hidden away," Black Berry answered, grinning. "And the truth is, J.C. owes me a good deal of cash and when I find him, I'm going to get it back . . . one way or another. And when I do, because you've been so nice to me, I'll give all I get from you to Blondie, so you can consider it as just a loan."

"I thought maybe it was J.C. you were really looking for. You're not going to shoot him, are you?"

"Does it matter?" Black Berry asked and began dressing.

Phyllis stared at him for a moment. "I have a thousand dollars under the bottom drawer of the chest in the corner," she said rolling her head toward the corner of the room.

"I'll take that as a no . . . that it doesn't matter to you," Black Berry said and smiled at her decision. "You know. I think I like you."

"And, if you promise not to harm Blondie," Phyllis continued in a serious tone, "I'll tell you where her loser husband might be—"

"It's a promise." Black Berry quickly answered.

"He's from Arizona. He owned a bar or a saloon or something in a small town called Upland, but pretty much gave it away before he met Blondie. I'm sure that's where he'd go."

"Gave it away? I heard once he'd lost a bar in a pool game."

"It's the same thing as far as I'm concerned."

"I thought it was just talk. The guy who beat him must have been a damn good player."

"They're all just worthless bums who took my daughter from me, nothing more," Phyllis said, watching him as he dressed.

"Are you sure he'd go back there?"

"It's his hometown. If he didn't come here, he has nowhere else to go."

Black Berry finished dressing then retrieved the ten one-hundred-dollar bills from the chest of drawers. He walked over to Phyllis and kissed her full on the mouth and while she couldn't see him, he reached for his pistol considering what would be his best course of action: a pillow to muffle the sound or just blast away and hurry out of town. However, he had a strange liking for her and was sure the feeling was mutual, and what if he did decide to come back? Does he want to burn this bridge too? He eased his hand from the pistol grip. "If I untie you," he said, "will you swear to give me an hour or two before you tell anyone I was here?"

"I'll never tell anyone." She looked him dead in the eye and smiled. "After all, you promised you'd be back."

Black Berry untied her hands, kissed both of her breasts, and walked out of the house, fully confident no one would ever know he'd been there, and sure that shooting her would have been a big mistake anyway.

Ten minutes after Black Berry left, Juan and José Hernandez rang Phyllis Straub's doorbell.

"Hello," she said. She was wearing a large bathrobe and holding a tumbler of wine. Her hair was a frizzy mess.

"*Buenos dias*," Juan answered and smiled. "There was an *hombre* here a bit ago. When he left, he lost his spare wheel and some tools to fix it with, which is very dangerous."

José had removed the limousine's spare tire and jack, held those up as proof, and smiled. His colossal teeth sparkled.

"Oh my," Phyllis said.

"We were going to follow him," Juan continued, "but by the time we gathered everything up, he was gone. If we knew where he was going, we could catch him and return these things."

"Arizona," Phyllis quickly answered. "He's headed to Upland, Arizona."

"*Gracias*," Juan said. "We will now find him before he gets to the highway."

"Please do," she said.

"We would expect he would do the same for us," Juan said.

"I'm sure he would," Phyllis answered.

José threw the stuff back in the trunk of the limousine and waved pleasantly.

Please hurry," she called to them as they quickly drove off.

Thirteen

J.C. decided that the boy was right. Why give the money away? Therefore, he refrained from gambling, not even a dollar for the slots or Keno. After a good night's sleep, another mighty breakfast, and a boat ride up the Colorado River to see the casinos from the river's side of the strip to satisfy their want to be tourist, they loaded up the Honda and squeaked across the bridge over the river into Arizona. From Bullhead City, they followed highway 68 to Kingman, and old route 66 until it petered out at Ash Fork, then on into Flagstaff via Interstate 40, the only logical route available.

In old downtown Flagstaff, they settled into a grand refurbished hundred-year-old hotel. Home of past presidents and gunslingers alike, according to the sign posted at the entrance. After another lavish dinner and hours of restful sleep in deep soft mattresses and crisp sheets, they were up enjoying the small but clean shower. When J.C. walked out sporting a clean-shaven face, Kid laughed. "No one will know who you are," he said. It was the first time that Kid had seen his father without whiskers.

"That's the idea, kiddo." J.C. rubbed his smooth face.

"And you look so young."

"That's also the idea." J.C. grinned.

Following a breakfast of eggs Benedict, Canadian bacon, and real orange juice, they got haircuts and shopped for new attire—modern and flashy and well fitting—and more of the necessities for taking care of their personal needs, including toothbrushes.

"Your mother's instructions," J.C. explained when Kid bulked.

They enjoyed the life of leisure and wealth until the long shadows of late afternoon stretched across the landscape and J.C. declared it time to move on. They packed the back seat with bags and boxes of their new garb and headed south, past tall pines, silvery aspens, and red rocks, past old mining towns, small horse ranches, and new summer homes. And shortly after the sun set, they rolled into Upland, ending the long days of engine whining, tire squealing, and seat squeaking—a symphony even Van Halen's *Runnin with the Devil* could not completely overcome. Before leaving Flagstaff, Kid tried to talk his father into buying a better car, but J.C. refused to consider such a hefty expenditure on the grounds that, since they didn't give it to the casinos, he now had better use for their newly found riches. "Maybe we'll do something reckless and buy ourselves a saloon," he said.

J.C. backed the Civic into a parking space on Mesquite Avenue with the town square behind them. In that position, they faced the infamous row of bawdy bars and saloons situated on the west side of the avenue between Rawhide and Horseshoe Streets. Saloon Row was an integral part of Upland's way of life and had been for as long as even the old timers could recall; it was ingrained into the very fabric of the locals' psyche. At the turn of the century, saloons of various sizes ringed the town square, but in 1904, a firestorm engulfed most of the buildings. Unperturbed and declaring themselves miners instead of firefighters, patrons of the saloons simply took their drinks across the street to the town square and watched the show. The Last Chance saloon was the only establishment on the west side of Mesquite Avenue to be spared. Remaining intact, it continued to serve liquor and whores to miners until midcentury when "whoring" was outlawed in Upland, though liquor still flows to this day.

J.C. was born there, in the upstairs apartment, he explained to Kid, nine months, give or take, after his father impregnated his mother in the back seat of a Mercury sedan parked across the street from Saloon Row, in front of the town square, and maybe even on the very spot in which they were now parked. Bobby Forkner packed up his Mercury as soon as he got the news of his impending offspring and headed to places unknown.

Twelve years after his birth, J.C. told Kid, his mother was knocked up again. This time in the back seat of a green something or other, across the street from the saloon, in front of the town square, and maybe even on the very spot in which they were now parked, by some rodeo cowboy who blew town as soon as she was out of his car. J.C.'s "sort of brother" was born nine months later, give or take.

Their mother named them both Forkner and raised them above the saloon. Later, she inherited the business when old man Hinkle died. Hinkle refused to pass the saloon to his son, who'd moved to Phoenix and showed no interest in it, or in him.

"That's the place, there." Kid pointed across the street. "That old building?"

The lap-sided two-story building was built in the mid 1800's on the corner of Mesquite Avenue and Rawhide Street. It has maintained its original two-hundred-year-old façade, including genuine double swinging bar doors, thick plank floors, and its own wraparound lean-to walkway that is still in use. Also original, and still in use is the wooden sign above the swinging door and has held steady its siren's call from miners of a hundred years ago to bikers and pool players today in carved faded yellow box letters:

LAST CHANCE
SALOON

"That's it," J.C. said. "We're home, kiddo. It hasn't changed in two centuries. Let's go find someplace to stay and come back tomorrow to see if anyone remembers me." He was about to drive away when an Upland police cruiser, a compact Ford, pulled up in front of the saloon. The cruiser's lights dimmed out and the door opened. A tall, broad-shouldered cop stepped out, stuck a wide brimmed cowboy hat, with the brim rolled upward, onto a full head of hair, and locked the door. He clipped the key ring on his equipment belt and disappeared into the saloon.

J.C. eased the Civic back into the parking space and turned off the engine. "See that officer?"

"Uh huh."

"That's sort of your uncle."

"A cop?"

"Hard to believe, but that would be my sort of brother."

"No kidding?"

"What if we go in and say hey?"

"Sure," Kid said and shrugged.

J.C. pulled a bottle from between the seats, uncapped it, and with a grandiose flair, drained the last drop. He opened the car door and stepped outside. The air was cool on a slickened face and stung old, tired eyes as he crossed the street with Kid following. J.C. paused at the wooden steps and squinted up and down the street. It all looked and smelled and felt like twenty, thirty, forty years ago.

He stepped up to the entrance and peered over the swinging doors, and there it was: the long dark walnut bar along the right wall with matching ornate back bar behind it, the mix of two and four top tables with high back walnut chairs in the middle, and a row of upholstered booths along the back wall; nothing had changed. He was ten again, learning to shoot extraordinary and astounding pool in the smoke and dust filled backroom, on a worn out nine-foot pool table that had been hauled up from St. Louis by wagon train. He was eighteen again, watching over a six-year-old brother while trying to hustle pool at a dollar a rack from the few miners still left in town. He was thirty again; forming the decision to leave Upland on that same pool table after his mother died and left the saloon to him. The decision to leave Upland would take him to fame and fortune, he'd hoped, and to a bigger and better life away from the pettiness of a small-town girl. But in the end, he'd simply snookered himself again by the liberal thoughts of youth and the pool playing luck of Hog Stevens.

Kid watched his father's nostalgic musing, and then asked, "Why'd you leave, Pop?"

"No *tuve alternativa*," J.C. answered, "I had no choice." He pulled a Lucky Strike from a rumpled pack and placed it between his teeth. "Come on inside kiddo, and I'll buy you a soda pop."

Fourteen

Fred "Hog" Stevens was born in Phoenix but moved to Upland as a boy when his father took a teaching job at Upland High School, a school that Hog dropped out of as soon as he turned sixteen. Within two months of becoming a dropout, he hooked up with a motorcycle gang and followed them to California on an old Harley *panhead* that he'd put together in his father's garage. He stayed with the gang until they robbed a gas station in Sacramento and the clerk pulled out a sawed-off shotgun and cut loose on them. He was "scared straight," he liked to say when he talked about it, which didn't happen often because he wasn't particularly proud of that part of his past. After the fiasco in Sacramento, he returned to Upland and lived with his parents until becoming a saloon owner.

Now, after fifteen years of operating the saloon by himself, Hog was ready to give it up for love. Dana Excell had ridden into his life on a Harley Low Rider. She rode solo on the motorcycle but traveled with a troop of bikers up from Phoenix who stopped at the saloon often for refreshments, lunch, pool, and smalltime rowdiness, as did many other bikers, especially on hot summer afternoons. Dana proved different from most biker chicks Hog had met—not meek, but subdued, tall and comparatively lean, with long, dark hair tied in a braided ponytail with a Harley fob that spanked her tight black leather pants as she walked. She generally wore a sleeveless shirt with a short black leather vest, showing not only her biker colors, but also a tattoo on her right arm that extended from wrist to shoulder. The tattoo inked in bright yellows, reds, and blues, mimicked the universe with the planets orbiting her arm. Her face, pockmarked from a rough adolescence, wasn't totally unattractive, not by Hog's standards anyway.

Hog, on the other hand, wasn't called Hog for no reason. He was a full six feet, six inches tall, extremely broad shouldered, solid stomach, and a thick burley neck.

"How much do you weigh?" Dana had asked on her fourth trip to Upland and the saloon.

"Don't rightly know," he'd answered.

"How could you not know?"

"I don't never weigh myself."

"Why not?"

"No need," he'd said, "I am what I am."

"And what are you?"

"In love," he'd joked, thinking of tattoos she might have in places most people wouldn't care to see.

And when she smiled and didn't run screaming to the other side of the room, he'd taken a deep breath and asked her if she'd be interested in doing something or other with him at some time or other.

"Like what?"

"What is it you enjoy?"

"I like bike riding, but mostly I like unexpected things. Surprise me."

He'd surprised her by rolling out his not yet restored 1970 V-Twin Super Glide that he'd traded the old panhead for. The Super Glide was in no better shape, however, but he liked the size and style. It was in bad need of paint, tires, and engine casing gaskets to stop the deluge of oil splatters but, as he'd hoped, she had been fully impressed. At first, they'd merely tooled around Upland, she on her Low Rider and he on his leaky Super Glide, but then started taking longer rides, making many stops for snacks and conversations.

Those trips revealed that Hog had won the Last Chance in a pool game fifteen years earlier when he slopped in the nine-ball on the ninth game of a race to five. He'd been lucky in that he called the nine-ball in a side pocket and then lost control of the cue-ball, which caromed off another ball and by chance into the nine, tapping it into the called pocket. The rules were that you call the ball and pocket, he explained, but not necessarily the route of the cue-ball, so he'd walked away with the prize once he paid a token two grand. He'd borrowed the money from his parents, and he'd made it clear to her that he'd paid it all back within the first year. Then he explained to her how there were nine games in a race to five.

At one point, Dana had revealed that she'd not always ridden solo. She and her "old man" wore the colors of *The Knights of Columbus* and had since before leaving Ohio. They had been instrumental in starting the Phoenix chapter. In the beginning, they'd received much grief from the Catholic organization of the same name, but true to their creed—any run in with the establishment was to be ignored until it went away—they'd ignored it, it went away. Then, more than a year ago, a drunk driver in a Cadillac Allante had wiped-out her old man, and she was expecting a sizable settlement by year's end.

She was Hog's kind of woman, and he now watched her from behind the bar as she chortled with her inebriated friends across the room. He never considered himself a jealous man but watching her with them was starting to hurt. Pangs of the heart, he figured, not knowing what that really meant. Maybe he should get it over with, and just flat out ask her to marry him. However, fearful that something that serious might frighten her away, he rejected the idea.

As he watched her with a forlorn look in his eyes, the twin doors of the saloon swung open and acting Police Chief Troy Forkner sauntered in. "Hi-ya, Hog," Troy said as he slid up to the ornate bar.

"Bud'n-a-bottle?" Hog asked as if it were one word.

"Make it a Light. Holly says I need to watch the expansion."

"How is she?"

"Pregnant."

"Sorry to hear that."

"Uh huh," Troy answered and downed half the beer.

The saloon doors swung opened again and both men turned to look. Silhouetted by the backlights of the town square, a youngster and an older man stood smiling. Both were dressed in casual sportswear, perfectly coordinated, and perfectly fitted.

The vaguely familiar looking man held his hands as if stroking a pool cue. "Anybody looking for an Eight Ball game?" he asked. A bent cigarette bobbed in his teeth.

"Son of a bitch," Troy said.

"Son of a bitch," Hog said.

"Son of a bitch," an old timer at the bar said

Fifteen

Dana tended bar for Hog as he joined Troy and J.C. at a booth at the far side of the room. Hog had given Kid a handful of red-marked quarters and invited him to play Pac Man on the only video machine in the saloon. "They're marked red, so I'll get 'em all back when the game is emptied," he informed the boy.

"Nice," Kid said, shrugged and eagerly began playing.

Hog placed three small liquor glasses on the table, opened a bottle of Jack Daniel's Old № 7, and poured. "Say when," he said to J.C., but stopped before the glass overflowed. "Can't you speak none?"

"I remember the glasses being bigger," J.C. said and picked it up. Liquid sloshed over his fingers as he gulped the whiskey down. "Don't you have any Wild Turkey?"

"Somewhere, I'm sure, but I prefer Tennessee whiskey," Hog said and poured Troy and himself a drink, not coming near the top of the glass.

"Humph," J.C. mumbled.

Hog positioned the bottle of Jack in the middle of the table where all could reach it. "That's a good lookin' boy you got there, J.C.," he said. "He looks just like Troy."

"That's a good decision the boy made," J.C. said, "not looking too much like his old man." This time he poured his own drink.

"So, brother, how the hell you been?" Troy asked.

"Drowning the liver, poisoning the lungs, not shooting pool for shit, the wife screwing me over for a young dick, and you're looking at a dead man because of it. Other than that, I'm doing good, how about you?"

"I'm thinking about quitting the cops and robbers thing, and I believe I'm getting married, but I'm not sure. I guess I'm just as screwed up as you are."

"I'll drink to that—" Hog held up his glass for a toast "—to the screwed up Forkner brothers."

All raised their glasses high then gulped down their drinks in agreement.

Hog refilled them. "And one more," he said and again raised his drink to Dana, who smiled at him from behind the bar. "To my woman," he said. "We plan on ridin' cross country, from here to Florida for sure and maybe back."

The brothers also raised their drinks, "To Dana," both said and emptied their glasses in a single swallow.

"Congrats, Hog," Troy said. "I didn't know you had it in you."

"You got that kind of money?" J.C. asked.

"Well, she ain't poor none, not for long anyways, and I plan on sellin' the saloon."

J.C. smiled and looked around. The room was dark and gloomy, with fifteen years of Hog's neglect. "It could use a major uplift," he said, "can't be worth much."

"More 'en you'd think," Hog replied. "But here's the thing. Considerin' how I came by it and all, I'd be willin' to give the Forkner brothers a hell of a deal. I mean easy payments and such. If either of you are interested, I'd talk turkey."

"It would have to be one hell of a deal," J.C. said. "And speaking of Turkey—" he held up his empty glass "I like Kentucky whiskey."

"I might be getting married," Troy repeated, avoiding the meaningless disagreement. "I suspect I'll be broke before long, so count me out."

"Just a thought," Hog shrugged and filled J.C.'s glass with Tennessee's Old № 7.

"It is an interesting thought, though," J.C. said. He raised the undersized glass to his mouth and brought it down empty. Then he fumbled in his pockets and fished out a crumpled, almost empty pack of smokes. His hands trembled slightly as he flipped open his old butane lighter and cranked the wheel. A two-inch flame torched the end of the cigarette. A cascade of light flashed from his pinkie ring. The ring had a solid silver band with a flat circular face of yellow gold depicting a nine-ball, with thirty-six small cut diamonds encircling it. Eighteen more diamonds of the same size formed the 9.

"Love the ring," Hog said.

J.C. laid his hand on the table for all to see. "I won it in Vegas from an Italian wannabe twelve or so years ago. I beat him nine racks to two, and when he couldn't pay the losses, I settled for some cash and the ring."

"I'll put this place up against the ring as down payment," Hog quickly responded, "right now . . . one quick game of Nine Ball."

"Four shots of whiskey in twenty minutes," J.C. said, "fat chance I'm in any condition to play."

"Since when did four shots slow you down?"

"I'm not as young as I used to be. Wait till I'm sober then maybe we'll play for something substantial."

"When would that be?" asked Troy. "I've got to say this, brother: you're pretty sorry looking. Even those new duds can't hide it. I can't imagine you've been sober for some time."

"You are what you settle for, boys," J.C. said, "and that's always an accumulation of your decisions . . . or indecisions as the case may be."

"Yeah, well it looks like you settled for dreadful," Troy said. "I mean, you're dressed pretty sharp and all, but—"

"Hell, bro, I came in for a drink and to show off my offspring over there. What's with all the bashing?"

"I'm with that," Hog said and poured another round of Jack. "So you're sayin' I'm a mountain cause I settled for it?"

J.C. took a small, dignified sip and carefully placed the glass in front of him. "You settled on being big when you were young. You made the decision long ago not to do anything about it, and because you settled for it, you stayed that way. As for me, I settled on being a drunk instead of a professional pool player. And Troy, well he settled on being with the police when he could've been something big like an airline pilot or doctor or lawyer or some such thing, but he settled on something less."

Hog rolled his eyes. "You were always the talker." He pushed himself from the table and lumbered across the room.

"I had to join the Air Force to survive after you bailed." Troy reminded his brother. "I discovered flying and fighting crime and stayed with it. That's the decision I made. I don't call it settling."

Hog ambled back with a triple order of hot wings. The Forkner brothers stared at the heaping platter.

"I'm gonna share," Hog said, and then yelled across the room: "Hey, kid, come and get your fingers greasy."

Several customers came and went as the four ate the spicy chicken remnants, mostly old timers and most remembered J.C., and patted him on the back, shook his hand, offered to buy drinks, and so on. They talked about Hog's remaining at the saloon all these years and his newfound love, and how incredibly lucky he was to have even found someone given his age, size, appearance, demeanor, and so forth. They went over Troy's problems with the town and the feds, and his possible upcoming nuptials, and Hog mentioned Troy's impending offspring, which spurred another round of drinks.

They danced around J.C. and his marital woes, however, until Troy finally asked, "So, big brother, what really brings you to town, and how long are you going to be here?"

"That old Honda out there boys, that's what brought me here," J.C. answered as if he were dead serious. "And the rest of my life . . . yeah, I'm sure that's close to right. I'm sure I'll be here the rest of my life."

Sixteen

"**Christ**. Christ O Mighty." J.C. mumbled after stroking the shot a skosh too hard while pocketing the five-ball, sending the cue-ball behind the seven, and hooking his next shot: a straight in on the six with a probable runout. He'd forced the shot trying to overcome the ruts in the worn thin billiard fabric.

They were playing on the antique King pool table in the back room of the old saloon. The game was Nine Ball with ten dollars on the nine-ball and five on the five-ball, each to be paid as the balls were pocketed.

J.C. accepted the Lincoln and handed it to Kid, who was acting as his banker. "He's becoming one of my favorite presidents," he told the boy and winked.

"When do I get to play, Pop?" Kid whispered, "I can beat this guy."

"Not now, son. These are catchup games, to be played by us old farts from Upland. Right now, you're the banker, and a damn good one at that, I might add."

They had moved into the pool table room at the request of some of the older regulars, wanting to see if J.C. still had the touch. He did not. In fact, he would have been embarrassed had he been clear-headed enough to be embarrassed. The fact he'd been awake for a day and a half also might have played into his lackluster performance, had he been sober enough to let it. The reality of why he was still in the game of course had everything to do with the total lack of skill of the others in the room.

They were now down to two players: J.C. and Howard "Jiffy" McGuire, the house painter. However, there was still a full complement of spectators. Troy, who'd already lost all the money he brought with him; Kid, who was doing a fabulous job watching his father's winnings; Hog, who kept the drinks flowing at two bucks a pop instead of playing; and three regulars, whose names J.C. couldn't remember, and who were now giving out unwanted advice. Others had retired to their homes or the bar, all shaking their heads at the lousy display of pool shooting, especially by their onetime local guru. They could recall long runs, perfect cue-ball control, and magical cut shots. They all knew, however, that life and time had a way of making waste of even the most magnificent.

Though normally an excellent player, Jiffy had always been an easy mark, easy to shark, J.C. recalled, but now he was holding his own—if not word for word, then certainly ball for ball, game for game, and drink for drink. Still, J.C. was up a hundred and fifty dollars overall and hoped Jiffy would be good for another fifty before he gave up the hunt.

In much need of repair, or at least a good cleaning, the room itself was dirtier than it needed to be, and a good deal smaller than J.C. remembered, with barely room for eight people including those playing. The six feet or so between the head of the table and the wall provided ample room for breaking, but spectators on the right side had to duck and sway to allow cue room for the players, an annoyance J.C. also had not remembered.

"Why don't you take care of the frigging table, Hog?" J.C. complained as he tried a safety and screwed it up.

"I had it covered a couple of years ago." Hog defended himself.

"That's obvious. Have you ever replaced the cushions?"

"Nobody plays on it much."

"No wonder," J.C. scowled as he watched Jiffy take the cue-ball *in-hand* and place it on the table for an obvious easy runout. "Christ, this is pitiful." He almost rapped the shaft of his Rambow on the table but stopped short of contact. Black Berry's blood had dried on and stained only a small part of the Irish linen wrap. The remainder had easily rubbed off the slightly bent forearm with the help of a whiskey-soaked napkin, and J.C. noticed a couple of two-inch hairline cracks emanating backward from the joint that were growing with play, but the cue performed well enough considering what it had gone through, which J.C. considered often. He wondered if Black Berry had survived the head bashing, and if anyone had yet bothered to bury Johnny Bishop, if indeed Black Berry had shot him. And he worried over how long it would be before the police started looking for him, if they'd simply walk through the front door and say, Tony Forkner, you're under arrest for the robbery of the Velvet Rail Family Billiard Center, or for the murder of Levi

Berry, alias Black Berry. Or the ultimate quirk of fate would be if his only brother had to arrest him.

"It's still for sale," Hog said.

"What?" Taken by surprise, J.C. looked up at him, fumbled in his shirt pocket for a smoke, pulled one out, and popped it in his mouth.

"If you think you can do better 'en me," Hog continued, "it's still for sale."

"Well hell, Hog. I think anyone could do better than you. But that don't mean I can afford to buy it since you haven't stipulated a price." He flipped the wheel of the butane and torched the cigarette, again light glittered from his pinkie ring. "And Christ O Mighty, you've let the place go to hell. It can't be worth much."

"I told you I'd give one or both of you Forkners a screamin' deal, cause of the way I won it and all. I mean you could have welched on the bet because I had no way of collecting, but you didn't."

"It's something you should consider, Pop," Kid said with wide eyed enthusiasm. "I like it here already."

"I may be able to help some," Troy agreed. "That is, if you do it before I get married. Assuming, of course, I get married. It would do the boy some good to have a place to settle. Hell brother, you and I grew up here, and at least one of us turned out okay."

"Humph," J.C. groaned.

"Come on, Pop," Kid said. "We may have enough money already."

J.C.'s head snapped sideways, and he glared at Kid. "Now boy, you know better than that," he said then

Mose Duane

scanned the room, "And you pecker heads will have to start losing more than an occasional small bill to me if you want me to talk about something of this magnitude."

Jiffy leaned over a shot, stroked the cue once and turned it loose on the cue-ball, the seven-ball fell. "Well if you do buy it," he said, "I have no intentions of helping you finance it." He scurried around the table, set up for his next shot, and was taking aim just as the cue-ball stopped spinning. Click, the eight-ball fell, and the cue-ball moved around the table setting up for a long nine-ball shot.

"If you slowed down a bit, you'd probably be a better than average player," J.C. said. "You play way too fast, like Fast Eddie Felson, maybe, but not nearly as good."

"That's why they call me Jiffy," Jiffy responded.

Several in the room snickered.

"That's not what I heard." Hog laughed.

"Yeah, your wife said it's because you finish in a *jiffy*," one of the spectators added.

"She said you never left it in long enough to impregnate her, and that's why you only have the one kid," someone else continued, and everyone laughed.

"How *are* Gertrude and the girl these days?" J.C. asked as Jiffy bore down on the nine-ball. Jiffy dogged the shot; the cue-ball lumbered forward and well-off target, which left the nine-ball—the money ball—hung up in the corner pocket.

"Screw you, Tony. I knew you couldn't go all night without mentioning her name."

"Just being cordial," J.C. said as he pocketed the nine-ball and a Hamilton.

"Screw all of you!" Jiffy hollered and slammed his cue onto the pool table and rushed out of the room. "Screw all of you."

"Does he still own a pistol?" J.C. asked, leaning on his Rambow for much needed support and probably putting a little too much weight on an already damaged cue.

"Says he practices every day, some target, but mostly quick draw stuff," Troy answered.

"Humph," J.C. said. "That's not good."

"And the girl's name is Trude," Troy said.

"Trude. Right. I knew that." J.C. answered.

Seventeen

Dana had let Hog know from the start that she wasn't going to live in a grubby apartment above the saloon, and if he ever wanted to see her innermost tattoo, he'd better comply with her wishes. Two days later, he'd bought a small house off Main Street. Though built sometime in the middle of the century it was one of the newer houses in the neighborhood and just a short walk to his parent's house, not that he ever walked it. It had a four-car garage built some forty years after the house and was the larger of the two buildings, big enough to store their bikes and the equipment Hog needed to repair his. The garage alone should've been enough to seal the deal. What really did it for Hog, though, was Dana's description of the tattoo: "It's a pixie," she'd said with an evil smile, "looking for a way out."

When Hog mentioned he'd moved out of the apartment in favor of Dana's wishes, J.C. pressed him to rent it on a temporary basis. One of Hog's stipulations: J.C. had to promise at least to think about buying the saloon back.

The apartment was of course where J.C. and Troy had been raised by their saloon owning mother, before, during, and after she'd given up on laying any "swinging dick" that came to town in a shiny car. To her credit, in J.C.'s eyes anyway, she'd never entertained in the apartment, which was probably what accounted for her propensity for back seats of automobiles. He often wondered if she'd been a prostitute or simply drawn to wandering, worthless men, but he never had any particular desire to find an answer.

"I thought they called him Hog because of his size," Kid said as they walked through the disheveled apartment for the first time.

"It could use a bit of tidying, that's for sure," J.C. said. "But all in all, it hasn't changed in twenty years."

"Looks more like a hundred."

"We'll set up camp here for a while and in a couple of days, once we get it shipshape, it'll be just like home. That is if we stay." J.C. rinsed the dust out of a water glass he found in a cupboard and poured himself a tall Wild Turkey 101 from the bottle he'd brought up from the storage area at the bottom of the stairs. "Ol' Hog 'll never miss it," he said and grinned. "Bring me your soda and I'll give you a sample."

"No thanks. I've tried it and I'll stick to Pepsi."

"Suit yourself."

The apartment had a small kitchen with wooden table and chairs, living room, and two bedrooms, one on either side of the only bathroom. "Do I get a bedroom, Pop?" Kid asked.

"All to yourself . . . this is home, boy." J.C. sank deep into the worn-out sofa, his mother's sofa, set his drink on an end table and stretched his legs across the coffee table. He pulled the small pistol from his pocket, made sure it was loaded but not cocked, and wedged it between the cushion and the arm of the sofa. "For safe keeping," he said and lit a cigarette, inhaled, and let the smoke out in perfect circles. "I have fond memories of this place and of my mother," he continued. And between drinks of whiskey and puffs of Lucky Strikes, he strolled down memory lane, informing Kid that his grandmother had been strict, but never overbearing, that she had insisted on her sons always getting better than a C on their report cards, though Troy never got below a B even when he sloughed off his homework. That there were always games and birthday parties, Christmas trees and holiday dinners, and Easter egg hunts and picnics across the street in the town square. And that, as long as he kept up his grades, she allowed him to sneak down the stairs to the pool table to play, and she only had two basic rules about that: he had to take Troy with him wherever he went, and neither were allowed in the saloon when it was open. The pool players, however, always made sure he and Troy got what they wanted, if he continued to play. The players couldn't come to grips with the fact that any kid his age could beat them at their own game, consistently. However, they continued to pay him hoping he would lose a game or two, which he did sometimes, he informed Kid, because he'd learned earlier on that you had to grease the wheels occasionally to keep them turning. He figured he had to give back around ten percent to keep the money wheel spinning.

"There's a good lesson to be learned there," J.C. said. "Never get greedy. Let them win sometimes and they'll always be there to contribute to your wellbeing. Most gamblers will lose a thousand to win a hundred and think they've accomplished something. Don't you be a gambler, son, be a player."

"Speaking of gambling, Pop, are we going to buy back the saloon?"

"How much do we have now?"

"Fifty-five thousand and seventy-three dollars, including what you won from the pool game," Kid quickly answered.

"Let's sleep on it."

Eighteen

Kid woke up as soon as the morning sun filtered through the mucky window above his bed. He could smell the grime and mildew of the forsaken room, and when his feet touched the floor, he could see his footprints in the dust. The undersized room emitted the dingy grayish color of things old, from the walls to the meager furnishing, which consisted of a chest of drawers, a dresser, and a nightstand (with a lamp that didn't work) next to the single iron bed. A closet with a missing door added to the dullness. None of that mattered, however, because it all now belonged to him—his own private bedroom. Impatiently, he unpacked the shopping bags and boxes of clothing they'd bought since leaving California and neatly arranged them in drawers and door-less closet. He even made the bed, pulling the old dusty sheets and blanket taut and fluffing the pillow on top.

The ancient wooden floor creaked as he crept through the living room to check on his father, who continued to wheeze and hack as he had through the previous night or morning or day, or whatever it had been, Kid had no idea of the time, only that it was now daylight.

He showered as quietly as possible and briefly, but longingly, thought of his mother as he brushed his teeth, wishing she were with them.

He dressed in cargo shorts, collared shirt, and white sneakers. All new, he reminded himself, not the kind of secondhand stuff he'd grown up with. He quietly picked

112

up his father's Rambow, crept down the stairs and to the pool table, much like his father had done countless times, years ago.

Finally, he was going to play on the legendary King pool table, the one that had made his father, according to his bragging anyway, a world beater pool player—a talent that should have carried him to riches and fame. Kid looked around the room and thought that sometimes his father suffered from delusional memories. Ghostly white cobwebs were so thick high in the corners they seemed to be the only thing holding the old room together, welding the patchwork of plastered walls to the molded tin ceiling. Both walls and ceiling were the same hue of dirty gray that engulfed the whole building. The concrete floor appeared painted with a path worn around the pool table, or maybe it was years of built-up dirt, with a path worn around the table. Maybe it was both. Kid figured he'd probably have to clean it someday no matter what it was. It seemed a fair trade for having a home with his own room.

He screwed his father's cue together, set it aside, and rummaged through a rack of rough house-cues until he found a relatively straight twenty-one-ounce Valley that he would use for a break cue. He racked all fifteen balls, and they broke in the distinctive, ear pleasing "crack." They scattered, wobbling around the uneven table favoring the left side, some barely rebounding from the age-old cushions. Today, he planned to break his high run record on a nine-foot table, though it would be tough with such neglected equipment.

"Hey kid," Jiffy McGuire said as he walked through the door from the saloon, "thought I heard someone in here."

Kid looked up and saw the ragged old man wearing the same paint splattered pants and shirt he'd been in the day before; his eyes were drooping orbs of red. "Hi," Kid said. "I didn't think anyone would be here yet."

"Been here a couple of hours."

"Long enough to have a drink or two, huh?"

"Hell kid, I started drinking at home. Where's the old man? I brung my own cue this time." He held up an old Gordon Hart Viking in his right hand. His left hand held a tall glass of whatever the drink of the moment was.

"Pop's still asleep," Kid answered.

"How about you, then, would you like some competition?"

"For fun?"

"Are you shitting me? Your old man got me for nearly fifty bucks last night, and I came to get my money back."

"You figure on getting it back from me?"

"I heard you say you could beat me. Let's play ten on the nine and five on the five, same as before."

"But you lost it to my dad, not me."

"Your old man would do the same to me, or my kid, and think nothing of it."

"Okay," Kid said, and trying to calm his nerves, picked up the Rambow and sighted down it to see which way the butt was now bowed. If you have to use a bowed cue, the bow always goes down, he recalled. "In that case, let's play Eight Ball at a flat five a game."

Jiffy balanced his drink on the four-inch ledge that circled the room and racked for Eight Ball. "It's your break, kid."

Kid broke, made the three-ball and, favoring the left side of the table, continued to run the next seven solid balls, including the eight in the side pocket. "Are we playing winner breaks?" he asked.

"Christ," Jiffy more than mumbled as he handed over a crumpled five-dollar bill. "Don't you know the damned rules? "We play loser breaks, you know, to make it more fair, so you rack this time."

Kid smiled and knew Jiffy was already irritated, so wouldn't be hard to beat. Kid racked the balls, his initial apprehension fading fast.

Jiffy failed to make a ball on the break. Kid took over, made four solid balls, and tried a safety. Jiffy made three striped balls, missed his next shot, and then Kid ran out for the win. He collected another five. "You sure got unlucky on the break," he said as he re-racked the balls. "Here, try again."

Jiffy broke and made the eight-ball.

"Boy, Mr. McGuire, you are unlucky."

"That ain't no loss, kid, not here anyway. We just spot the eight and continue to play."

"Uh huh," Kid said, "But I get ball *in-hand*, right?"

"I'm not sure that's right."

"Well it's your rules. Either I do or I don't."

"Okay, okay, whatever."

Kid made two balls but failed to break open a cluster and knew he couldn't run out, so made an adequate safety, leaving Jiffy in a position where he couldn't make firm contact with his object ball, so he too made a safety. Kid made another safety.

"You know," Kid said while Jiffy attempted his second safety, "it's a good thing I won the first two games, because I didn't have any money to start with."

Jiffy missed his safety. "Goddamn it," he yelled and cracked his cue over the end rail, sending splinters flying.

Kid cleaned the debris from the table, proceeded to run seven striped balls, and then sank the eight.

"You're just like your goddamned old man," Jiffy said as he handed over another five spot and picked up splinters of his cue shaft. "Always talking, always needling. You can't just play pool."

"I'm sorry," Kid said as he re-racked the balls. "I was just making conversation. There are some straight house cues in the rack in the corner, if you want to continue to play."

"You do know he don't want anything to do with you, don't you?"

"What does that mean?"

"Your goddamned old man, goddamn it, he don't care for you none, he don't care for nobody, but who he sees in a mirror."

"Pop always said you gotta like yourself if you want anybody else to like you, so I guess he likes himself, sure enough."

"He told me and Troy and Hog that he wished your mama had kept you instead of palming you off on him."

"You're just trying to shark me because that's what you think I was doing to you."

"Think so? Well, he used to be my best friend until he started screwing my wife. Knocked her up and left town and palmed his kid off on me to raise. Did you know you had a sister, kid? Huh? Did you know that?"

Kid just stared, eyes wide, mouth agape.

"And he didn't care enough to stay and face me; didn't have the balls to tell her he didn't care for her none, neither. Then he shows up here all high and mighty with his fancy expensive clothes, wanting to know how they are, and such shit."

"I don't know much about what Pop did back then, but I know—"

"It's all a lie, son," J.C. said and stepped into the room, half a cigarette bobbing in his teeth. He'd found his bag of "fancy expensive clothes" and had dressed accordingly but had apparently not found his razor or comb. "Except the part about his wife, that is. She came on to me; said Jiffy there couldn't do her any good."

"Screw you, Tony! You piece of shit," Jiffy hollered. "Why don't you get out of town? Get out of my life."

"Humph. I may be moving back for good," J.C. said. "Now come on into the saloon, boy, and I'll buy you an egg or something while we discuss such a reckless thing as maybe buying this place, and to prove I don't want to palm you off on anyone." He rubbed Kid's short-cropped hair. "I might sell you, but they'd have to offer at least a couple of fresh new Franklins."

Kid smiled at the attention, but asked, "Do I have a sister?"

"Well it's kind of hard to say, son. But I wouldn't bet on such a thing," J.C. answered.

"I say you're a piece of shit that don't care for nobody but yourself," Jiffy continued.

"Now let me think on that for a sec," J.C. said and deliberately extracted the stub of a cigarette from his mouth, flipped it to the floor, and ground it out with his new shoes. He perched on the pool table and allowed his feet to dangle, fumbled through a couple pockets until he produced a crinkled pack of Lucky Strikes, extracted another cigarette, cranked the wheel of the butane, and set the tobacco afire. "Well, thinking back on what I might and might not have done, I can say I never wanted to be a piece of shit." He blew a couple of smoke rings. "But I must admit, sometimes opportunities lent themselves in such a passionate way that I couldn't turn away, couldn't exactly say no, if you know what I mean. But as to the boy having a sister, I couldn't rightly say as to if he does or doesn't."

"I have a mind to break my cue over your head," Jiffy said, holding up what was left of the cue he'd just broken over the table. He was starting to cry.

J.C. grinned at the old sobbing painter now holding half a cue as if it were a bat. "Now I know from recent experience you can cause serious damage with a cue, Jiffy."

"You mean what's left of it," Kid added.

"Now son, don't you go antagonizing him. He's already building one hell of a grudge against me. There's no reason he needs to start on you."

"Look at you." Jiffy cried as he talked to Kid. "You're going to be just like him, thinking you're God's gift to the pool table, God's gift to women, God's gift to the—"

"Well, if I'm a gift from God," J.C. said, "I don't know why I ended up like this, and as far as women go, I don't know about the boy there, but I've had my share. Used to be they'd throw themselves at me, thought I was handsome or some such thing."

"I know your story," Jiffy said. "You screwed every other girl over twelve in town."

"Cowshit."

"No, bullshit, that's what you'd tell them, just plain ol' bullshit. Any kind of bullshit you could come up with to get them to yank their little panties past their snatchs."

"Horseshit. That's what it is, horseshit I only wish was true. I would think back on such encounters and smile, and crow a little, if it were true."

"You started in on Gertrude when she was only twelve, not even legal."

"That's not true, either. Seems she was more like fourteen, fifteen maybe. There's a difference."

"See, you been screwing my wife for years. I knew it all along," Jiffy cried and swung his cue at J.C. The cue no longer had a shaft, so the swing missed by a foot and a half.

J.C. ducked by reflex, shifted his weight, and tumbled off the table and onto the floor, scuffing his new shoes and soiling his new trousers. "What the hell you doing?" he yelled as he pulled himself to his knees. He plucked a two-ball off the pool table with his left hand and threw it. The ball missed Jiffy by ten feet, bounced off the hard, thick plastered wall, and dribbled across the floor.

"You throw like a goddamn pussy," Jiffy said. "I always knew you were a goddamn pussy."

Hog pushed his large frame through the door. "Jesus, what the hell's goin' on in here?"

"He admitted to screwing my wife," Jiffy cried. "He finally admitted it."

"Of course, he did, but that was years ago, Jiffy. It was before you were even married, my God."

"No sir, he done it after we were married too . . . knocked her up too, sure as hell."

"Even so, it was still a long time ago," Hog said.

"More than once," J.C. said and laughed. "Maybe I'll come by tonight and see how she's doing. Maybe I'll go see how my daughter is doing too—"

Jiffy launched his cue, presumably at J.C., but it tumbled sideways and crashed through a window that had been painted over years earlier.

"Didn't even know that window was there," Hog said and grinned.

"Talk about throwing like a pussy," J.C. said.

After a moment, Jiffy walked toward the door, shoulders hunched, head drooped and shaking. "I don't know," he said, "I just don't know anymore." He walked past Hog and out the door.

"I need a drink," J.C. said and, wobbling, led the way to the bar.

Nineteen

Billed as the *Region's Rowdiest Rodeo,* the Upland competition had been around since the late 1800s. The show included most "ball busting" events like wild horseracing, saddled bronco riding, steer wrestling, bareback bronco riding, roping, and bull riding. "It was the kind of sport," according to J.C., "that attracted young good-looking bucks with hard heads and hard peckers, and that attracted young good-looking does with wide-open eyes and wide-open thighs."

Some years back, the organizers of the rodeo decided the "ladies" of the county should also participate in the bounty of prizes and trophies so introduced the woman's barrel racing event and the crowning of the Upland Rodeo Queen. It was that pageant that had lured Holly Garcia to Upland, by way of rodeo star Tex Bowman. And Holly Garcia was the reason J.C., Kid, and Troy now relaxed in the grandstand of the Upland Rodeo arena.

On Troy and Holly's recommendation, they'd all met for breakfast at Jack Watson's fine restaurant and coffee shop at the Upland Airport before going to the arena. Even Hog and Dana had shown up on their bikes before riding off to open the saloon. They'd pushed two of the four top tables together in front of a picture window, which gave them all a magnificent view of the runway. While watching the seemingly never-ending array of airplanes landing and taking off, J.C. had marveled at the odd mix of interests of the six people that were present. They were bikers, rodeo rider, police officer/pilot, kid with an unknown future, and a down and out pool player, all sitting around the table eating biscuits and gravy, eggs—over easy, over medium, scrambled—grits, pancakes, coffee, tea, milk, and orange juice, in some combination or another. What amazed him the most, he'd said, and everyone had agreed, was the one thing they all had in common: they were family and friends clinging to the possibility of that being their last chance for happiness. And happiness—or the illusion of such a thing, the intangible that had eluded him most of his life, even in marriage—was starting to creep into J.C.'s psyche.

The trio of two brothers and a son now had seats in the front row of the grandstand of the rodeo arena, behind the horsemanship clinic judge's box. They watched Holly, dressed in an all-white Wrangler cowgirl outfit, on a beige filly named Chance that belonged to Tex Bowman. At her bidding—an imperceptible tug at the reigns—Chance moved left then right, pulled up, backed up, broke into a full gallop, pulled up again, backed up again, left, right, big left turn, full gallop, pulled up in front of the judge's box, lifted a front hoof, and bowed. All this while Holly held a blank sponsor's flag that flew overhead on the long staff booted at the saddle. The clinic was held early to prepare the contestants for the actual horsemanship competition to be held the following week.

"She's a real beauty, Troy," J.C. said.

"Without doubt." Troy smiled.

"And Holly's not bad to look at either."

"Ha-ha."

"So, brother, she's the one that's finally going to lasso you, huh?"

"I know I said I was getting married, but the truth is—"

"You're scared shitless."

"That about sums it up. You know, is she the right one? And, as you so aptly put it, would I be settling?"

"Well, you don't have to tie any knots these days, you know. Nobody gets run out of town anymore for dwelling together, and plenty of women would just as soon shack up for a while as permanently end up with some short barreled quick shooter."

"I don't think that's the problem," Troy said grinning.

"I know, you're a Forkner." J.C. chuckled along with his brother, crushed a cigarette butt underfoot, and put a flame to another.

"Boy, some of those girls sure are cute," Kid said almost on cue. He'd been keenly watching the younger girls commanding their horses through the clinic, all doing a routine similar to Holly's.

"Lord help us, we have another one," Troy said.

"Chip off the old block." J.C. laughed.

Kid looked embarrassed but couldn't hide his smile.

"They're all cute, son, as you are destined to find out in a couple of years. They're all cute."

"Some more than others," Troy added.

"All cute and waiting for you, son."

"I think Holly's real cute too," Kid said, his eyes wide, his voice serious.

"Damn, J.C., I think I have some serious competition." Troy elbowed his brother. "You better keep your son in check."

"A branch off the old family tree, without doubt." J.C. laughed again.

The boy's face turned red. "But she's too old for me. She's older than most of the other girls."

"This is her one and only chance to make the pageant," Troy said. "Last year she hadn't been a resident long enough and next year she'll be past the age limit."

"Then I hope she wins."

"She still needs a local sponsor, or she can't even qualify. That's why she flew a plain white flag."

"Well—" Kid gave it a quick thought "—since this is her last chance and her horse is named *Chance* and the saloon is the *Last Chance*, shouldn't Hog sponsor her?"

"That boy is always thinking," Troy said.

J.C. agreed. The saloon would sponsor her, and he didn't care what Hog might have to say about it. She would fly the Last Chance banner. It would be perfect.

Satisfied, Kid wandered over to the edge of the grandstand where the younger crowd had lined up against the retaining fence to watch the proceedings.

J.C. pulled a slow draw of smoke into his lungs, let it escape in four doughnuts. He was feeling content. Life with family and friends. That was worth settling for. "You know, getting married, that's the one thing I always swore I'd never do," he said. "Then young Blondie bounced into my bed, and the next thing I knew Kid was on the way, so I settled little brother. Under the guise of responsibility, I suppose, but I settled, nonetheless. I settled for a meaningless job, and a meaningless life, though I always wanted more."

"More?" Troy asked. "You had a beautiful wife and have a great son."

"I blamed Blondie and the boy for holding me back. I wanted to roam the country and . . . I wanted what Blondie is now going after: the travel, the tournaments, the big wins. At first, I was pissed at her for leaving me and the boy, but now . . ." he stopped and, misty eyed, watched his son.

"But now?"

"Christ O Mighty, Troy. Now I hope she makes it. You know, to the big time. She has the game. I'm going to miss her, but I hope to hell she makes it big."

They watched several more girls perform, some as well as Holly, some less so, and they watched as Kid struck up conversations with others his own age and a young brunette in a cowgirl hat seemed particularly interested in him.

"You know, Troy, if something happens to me, I want you to take care of him for me until Blondie shows up."

Troy studied his brother for a moment. "What's going to happen?"

"I'm in bad shape. You said so yourself."

"Don't screw with me, Tony. Is there something I should know?"

J.C. mulled the question for a second. "Not really, but is that something you can do for me?"

"Kid will always have a home if he wants it. He kind of reminds me of us when we were that age."

And glossing over what might or might not happen in the near future, they reminisced about their own childhood days romping around the fairgrounds dressed like their favorite rodeo stars and looking mostly for young ladies dressed in cowgirl boots and short skirts. They laughed and carried on for longer than two sober people should be allowed, but eventually grew hungry, and "damn" thirsty, and J.C. had to declare it a morning before his son disappeared into the stables with a young brunette hanging on his arm. He pushed himself up and onto the walkway and motioned for Kid to follow.

"Is she the best I can do?" Troy asked.

"Don't know why you would want to take advice from such a wreck of an old fart," J.C. answered and flipped the last of a smoke under the bleachers, "but here's something to ponder: maybe she'd be the one settling."

Twenty

Troy watched J.C. and Kid leave then wandered out and around to the backside of the arena where the staging area and stalls were located. He'd considered walking over earlier, but still felt uncomfortable seeing Holly with the rodeo cowboy.

Tex and Holly were standing beside Chance. He joked and laughed while she brushed down the horse. Troy figured Tex, to his credit, had kept his promise and hauled Chance down from Montana so four or five of his girlfriends—or ex-girlfriends or whatever—would have a horse to ride in the pageant. Each girl had agreed to pay a share of the feed and stall bill, but Troy imagined Tex's fringe benefits would still be substantial.

Troy watched them for a moment. She seemed so happy, so into the cowboy. Troy lowered his head, turned, and walked away.

He drove to the airport; the one place he always went to be alone. There, he rolled the Waco from its covered tie down, and somberly walked around it checking the things that needed to be checked: guy wires, tight; fabric, tight; engine oil, full; fuel tank, full. All that he did more or less mindlessly, not necessarily thinking of the aircraft, but of Holly and what her story was. He climbed into the cockpit and fired up the engine. The powerful seven-cylinder radial roared to life. He called the control tower for special clearance, and a female controller gave it to him. He'd been around long enough to know all the controllers by name, and they certainly knew him.

"Thanks Beth," he said. "Keep an eye on me."

Beth McDonald was a short, round girl, and "cute as a button," as his mother would have said, with bright blue eyes and an endless smile. He'd seriously dated her four or five years back, but unlike Nina Miller, the only other girl he'd been serious about, he was the one who'd gotten cold feet and walked away. He smiled thinking about her and wondered why.

"Give it hell," Beth said.

The Waco was a tail dragger, and he could not see directly forward so in an S pattern, he snaked the plane to the runway, at the same time checking the engine magnetos and instruments to make sure all functioned in the normal range.

"Wah-co 73 Romeo, cleared for takeoff," Beth informed him as he turned onto the runway.

He lined up with the centerline by putting an equal amount of pavement on each side of the nose. Full throttle brought the tail up almost instantly and allowed him full view ahead. He pulled the nose off the runway at 55. The plane accelerated to 65 and, ever so lightly, he kept back pressure on the stick to keep the speed constant, and the Waco climbed. He turned crosswind then downwind still climbing and leveled off at 1200 feet turning base. He throttled back as if to land but pushed the stick forward to lower the nose and gain speed. The runway filled the windscreen as velocity built, as the plane nosedived toward the ground, back through 800 feet, 600, 400, 200 and then, at the last second, Troy hauled back on the stick, pushed the throttle full forward, and soared skyward, almost vertically. He did two quick snap rolls to the right as the engine yowled, before the plane finally, but briefly, suspended in midair, hanging on the prop as it clawed furiously for lift. Then the bottom fell out and the plane slipped backward. Troy yanked the throttle to idle and allowed the nose to slide over the left wing sending the plane earthward again, this time in a wing over wing spin. One thousand feet, 800, 600, 400, 200, and as smooth as glass he pushed forward on the stick, full rudder, full opposite aileron, and then heaved back on the stick. The plane leveled just above the centerline stripes, pulled up and thundered away from the airport. Troy spoke into his mike, "If I could handle myself around women like that, I'd be a happy man."

"I'm here," was the response from Beth and Troy smiled again.

Of course, flying was a skill to Troy, like driving a car or playing tennis or golf. Anyone with a modicum of intelligence could learn. To truly master an airplane, however; it must become an extension of you. It must react almost without physical manipulation, as if thought alone was in control. Troy learned to fly in the Air Force, when he was a much younger man, when skills drilled into his brain by the best instructors in the world, were easy to learn and retain. His aircraft did what he wanted, when he wanted, not the other way around.

Flying over fields, rivers, and mountains, Troy thought about Beth. She also received her training as a controller in the Air Force, which gave them that in common. She was a local, down-home girl, born and raised in Upland, and he knew her father well—he owned a service station on old road 79, out close to the highway. Beth wasn't going anywhere; she was here to stay, so why did he fall for a girl as flashy and flighty as Holly?

The weather looked worse from the air than it did on the ground. Dark clouds far to the north showed signs of virga. Troy headed for them. Half an hour later he was over the Grand Canyon and only five hundred feet below the clouds. The rain began to splatter the windscreen and into the cockpit, it felt cool and clean on his face. There were only four corridors allowed by the FAA in which a VFR plane could cross the canyon. Troy knew them by heart, but only used two: The Zuni Point corridor he liked for northbound travel with a minimum altitude of 11,500 feet, and the Dragon corridor he used for southbound travel with a minimum altitude of 10,500. He loved flying over the canyon. It was a place to get away, a place to be completely alone, a place to think. "Think about what?" he asked himself. "Holly?" She drove him insane. "Beth? Hum, maybe, and what about Nina?"

Nina, like Beth and most of the women he'd dated, was a local, hometown girl. He knew her past, knew and respected her mother, and her father who was a doctor in town. Both Nina and Beth were girls he could relate to and was certain that if they hadn't left town by now, their home would always be here. Holly, on the other hand, was not from Upland or even Arizona, and she had a sordid past. One he wasn't sure he even wanted to explore, especially when he thought of the cowboy. He didn't even know her parents, for Christ's sake, didn't know if she even had parents, or a family for that matter. How would he? She never spoke of them. He wondered if she would soon tire of Upland. Would she soon tire of him? Did any of it really matter to anyone, or was it simply an exercise in self-imposed frustration? Was he simply "scared shitless" of marriage as his brother had so expressively suggested.

"Marriage," he loudly spoke to himself, "is that your problem?"

He put the plane into a lazy barrel roll as he crossed the canyon through the Zuni Point corridor, all the while thinking of Beth or Nina, not Holly. He made a wide sweeping left turn over Saddle Mountain and headed back across the canyon through the Dragon corridor. He made two snappy aileron rolls, snappy but smooth, and then turned toward home before—like marriage—the clouds pinned him in completely.

Pilots, Troy knew, were always judged by their landings. A good pilot never got lost, never strayed into bad weather, never ran low or out of fuel. A good pilot could execute excellent formation flying, pinpoint bombing runs, and precision aerobatic maneuvers, but if he bumped the runway during a landing, non-pilots instantly labeled him a poor pilot, not worthy of his certificate. Therefore, during training, Troy practiced landings, coming in high sometimes, slipping the plane, one wing severely lower than the other, and greasing the runway on one wheel or, often, he flared the nose up and touched all three wheels as the plane stalled to a perfect three-point touchdown. Now, as he returned to Upland, he refused to let the plane bounce and barely noticed when the wheels skimmed to the runway, in a perfect two wheels landing, and thought, if only Holly was that easy to handle.

"When do you get off work?" he asked into his headset mike as he taxied to the tie downs.

"I have a lunch break in fifteen," Beth responded.

"Buy me a cup of coffee?"

"It would be my pleasure."

Beth hadn't changed, still bright eyed with a pleasing smile. "What's up?" she asked as she slid into the booth opposite Troy. A cup of coffee was already sitting on the table. She picked it up and blew over the rim.

"Feeling blue," Troy said. "How've you been?"

"I couldn't be better," she answered. "Are you on the rebound?"

"What?"

"I heard you've been with some cowgirl named Holly."

"Nina?" he asked. Sometimes he was amazed at how small of a town Upland really was.

"Yeah, she told me. It wasn't supposed to be a secret, was it?"

"Not really. Does it matter to you?"

"Some, I suppose."

"I'm thinking about calling it off."

"I heard she's pregnant."

"Yeah, that's what I hear."

"Think about what you want, Troy, but I don't think you're going to call it off. Not for Nina and certainly not for me," she said with a hint of sadness.

"Yeah, I suppose you're right," he said. "I'm sorry."

"Nothing to be sorry about, life goes on. Now buy me some lunch." She smiled big and bright. "There's no reason we can't be friends."

They talked while she ate, discussing life in a small town as compared to life in the Air Force. Both deciding that they were where they wanted to be, in Upland, at the airport eating lunch and drinking coffee with someone they liked, in their case ex-lovers for sure, but now friends and nothing more.

"You have to tell her you love her." Beth said sounding cheerful, but her expression didn't show it. "You can't expect her to read your mind."

"Why not? I know she loves me. She didn't have to tell me."

"But she did, right?" Beth said. "And I'm sure more than once."

"More than once, I'd say."

"There you go, that's what a girl wants to hear, and often. Now it's your turn, reciprocate."

Troy left feeling better after having talked to Beth. A woman's perspective, he supposed, was what he needed. He drove back to the rodeo grounds. Holly was nowhere around, but Tex was still there, now talking to a well-endowed redhead.

"Have you seen Holly?" Troy asked.

Tex gave him a long, hard stare. "You must be Troy."

"Troy Forkner," Troy extended a hand and Tex responded. His shake was firm but not confrontational.

"She said she was going home to look for you," the redhead said and smiled broadly, her green eyes twinkling. "I can see why."

Troy returned the smile, took a step to leave then turned back. "Would you consider selling the horse?" he asked Tex.

"It would be easier than hauling her back to Montana," Tex said, "and as far as I'm concerned, she and Holly belong together."

Twenty-One

Of course, after leaving the fairgrounds, J.C. and Kid returned to the saloon. They'd made it to the pool table where Kid amused himself playing a couple of hapless fans of the thirteen-year-old wonder for a sawbuck—five on the five and five on the nine. Remembering forty years ago, two old-timers wanted to call Kid, Tony, before being reminded in what time zone they now lived. One newcomer that caught J.C.'s eye, a short, stout-looking, Mexican, was overdressed to be a Last Chance regular, but Kid seemed to be handling him just fine. J.C. wasn't worried about the guy being a hustler, someone who could do damage to the kid's ego, not to mention wallet, in short order.

The old pool table appeared to suit the boy's game as he won match after match, missing only hard shots and never miscuing or dogging and always maintaining excellent control of the cue-ball. If you controlled the cue-ball, you controlled the game—and life. J.C. had instilled that tidbit of J.C.-ism into the kid's head long ago and knew the boy had learned it well. He'd also warned Kid that the game always spun your way when there was no pressure, when you were playing for beers, or small change, or points, the balls simply rolled the way you wanted. Put on some pressure though, add a large bill or two to the pot, and Lady Luck could and would close her eyes to you in an instant.

J.C. was sure, however, that Kid had the intelligence and grit it took to overcome The Lady and her quirkiness by keeping the game-stealing pressure at bay. He was convinced that the boy was going to be a much better player than Blondie, and maybe even better than he had been.

Leaving Kid to take care of business on his own, J.C. gingerly slid through the door to the bar. Beaming with pride, he told Dana that the youngster was going to be good, a world beater no doubt.

"Just like his father," Dana said as she poured him a drink.

"Where's Hog?"

"At home working on that pile of parts he calls a bike."

"I thought you liked his motorcycle."

"I do . . . when it runs. He's sitting on a heap of money. I wish he'd just go buy a new Harley so we can split before winter gets here."

"He's got that kind of cash, huh?"

"Are you kidding me? He hasn't spent a dime in fifteen years. He's got it."

"And he's really going to move away?"

"Lord no. He just wants out of the saloon owning business. Upland is his home; he's not leaving. We just want to go on *the big ride* before it gets too cold. And, knowing him, he'd probably come back here and work for you when we're done roaming. That is if you buy the place."

"Any wedding bells planned?"

Dana rolled her eyes. "I think I'm done with marriage, but Hog and I get along great, and I love it here too, so we'll probably just hang together."

J.C. lit a Lucky Strike, filled his lungs, and rolled the whiskey around in his glass. "Any idea when school starts?"

"I'd say a month or so ago," Dana answered, showing a smile of approval. "But you can probably still get Kid enrolled if you're thinking about staying too?"

"You never know what I might do, but I like the idea of Kid staying here . . . let me see the phone."

Dana hoisted an old black, rotary phone from beneath the bar and placed it on top, in front of J.C. "The more the merrier," she said.

J.C. fumbled through his wallet, pulled out a list of numbers, dialed one, got no response so dialed another. Johnny Bishop answered with a muted "Hello."

"Johnny? Is that you, you old fart? Are you still alive?"

"Son of a goddamn bitch," Johnny answered. "Is that really you?"

"Black Berry said he shot you," J.C. answered.

"Well, I sure as hell thought he would've shot *you* by now."

"Why? Did you tell him where I went?"

"Not me. But the guy I was playing pool with the day you left, you know, Eddy, the idiot in the blue shirt."

"What about him?"

"Well, he repeated everything you said, like he was a goddamned tape recorder or something. Then Black Berry shot him dead, deader than my wife, and she's been in the ground more than thirty years. Shot him right here in my house, deader than dead I tell you."

"Jesus Christ, Johnny . . . and he didn't bother you?"

"Hell no, I bolted, ran like a terrified rabbit with his pecker hanging out. He came looking, but I hid pretty good."

"What did the guy tell Black Berry?"

"He shot Stony too. You know, the pawn shop guy. At least they think it was him who done it. But I'd bet a stack of C-notes it was him."

"Johnny, what did the Eddy tell Black Berry?"

"That you were going to California to see your in-laws."

"Did he say what town?"

"Oh, yeah, where Blondie was from . . . Bakersfield I think."

"Bayfield?"

"Probably . . . yeah, that's where she's from all right."

"Shit. Was he going there?"

"Of course, he was. But listen to this, the police ain't only looking for him for killing those guys, but by God, I told them he was the one who blew up *my* safe and stole *my* money, so they ain't looking for you. And I told them that, by God, he stole all *my* pool cues too, and they ain't looking for Blondie neither."

"You did good, Johnny. Christ O Mighty, you did good. Have you called the insurance people yet?

"They already been here too. They're going to replace all *my* money—ten thousand, I told them—and pay me for all *my* cues—another ten grand. Ain't that a kick in the ass?"

"You're amazing, old man. Take care," J.C. said and hung up. He knocked back his whiskey but wasn't sure what brand Dana had poured him. "Christ. Christ O Mighty," he mumbled as he dialed Phyllis' number.

"Hello." She answered on the first ring, sounding inebriated.

"Phyllis?"

"Hey, you're not dead yet?"

"Is Blondie there?"

"Why? Did she leave you again?"

"Listen Phyllis, Blondie's in trouble."

"If she's in trouble, I'm sure it's your fault."

"I know, but she and some young prick stole this guy's stuff and sold it, and then took off. And the guy's looking for her."

"Where's Junior?"

"He's okay. He's with me."

"I want to talk to him."

"He's in the back room playing . . . listen, the guy's name is Levi Berry and he's looking for her. Has he contacted you?"

"No. Let me talk to Junior."

"Phyllis, listen to me. He's sometimes called Black Berry. He may want to do Blondie harm, and I need to know if he's been there."

"No. No J.C's or Kids or Hogs or Blackberries or Strawberries or Mulberries, I swear you guys and your stupid nicknames. Can't you just call each other by your given names?"

"Not now, Phyllis."

"If Junior is there like you say, why can't I talk to him?"

"Damn it, Phyllis, this is serious stuff."

Silence.

"Phyllis."

Silence.

"Shit. Hold on, I'll get him."

J.C. lumbered to the pool table room and told Kid to come and talk with his grandmother and see if anyone had been there looking for them.

"Grandma?" Kid asked as he put the odd receiver to his ear.

"Junior? Are you all right?"

"Sure. Dad's with me."

"Where's your mother?"

"Chicago, I think. Playing pool."

"Chicago? Who'd she go with?"

"Some guy named Rabbit. They took Johnny's pool cues and ran off. Mom told me to stay with dad while she's gone."

"You be a good boy for me, okay? And if you need anything, you call me, okay? And if you need a place to stay you call me, okay?

"Okay, okay, okay," Kid answered.

"I love you," she said. "Now, let me talk to your father again."

Kid shrugged and handed the receiver to J.C. "Love you too, grandma," he yelled back at the phone as he left.

"Phyllis," J.C. now spoke softly into the receiver.

"Why don't you send him out here to stay with me for a while?"

"Okay, I think that's a good idea." He watched Kid duck back into the pool table room. "When we get settled in, I'll put him on a bus or something. But right now, I need to know—"

"There was a guy named Billy something or another here looking for Blondie."

"What did he want?"

"He wanted Blondie."

"Phyllis . . . what did he want Blondie for?"

"He owes her some money—a thousand dollars— and he wants to pay her . . . and he said you owe him money too, and he said he wanted it back, and—"

"Can you describe him for me?"

"Well, yes. He was a pleasant, handsome man, dressed like a cowboy. And he had a terrible black eye."

"Christ. Did you tell him where we might be?"

"How would I know where you are?"

"I'll send Kid out as soon as I get a chance." J.C. said, smiled, and lowered the receiver onto its cradle.

Twenty-Two

Black Berry didn't have to make a complete trip around the town square before spotting the Honda Civic. At first, he wasn't sure it was J.C.'s, but the California CUE BALL license plate J.C. had always been so braggingly proud of was a dead giveaway. Black Berry figured that the plate alone should've been reason enough to put a hole through his heart long ago. The Civic was facing away from the park. Black Berry followed suit and backed the Speedster into a no-parking space beside the old Civic. It was the only empty spot along the street.

A crowd laughed and hooted beneath the trees of the town square. They were behind him so were of little interest. Across the street, he could see the row of brick buildings housing bars and taverns on the street level with names like Downtowner, Wagon Wheel, Red Dog, and, looking lost as if straight out of a western movie, the Last Chance saloon sitting on the corner. He figured if he waited long enough J.C. would walk out of one of them.

He had barely settled in when a squad car slowly drove past. The officer made eye contact with him then looked his car over but continued on his way. Black Berry kept an eye on the officer as he turned the corner at the end of the block. Choosing safe over sorry, he slowly eased into the flow of traffic and made his way to the opposite side of the town square where he spotted the Grande Hotel and promptly pulled behind the two-story brick structure. He parked, concealed his small vehicle between a dumpster and a neglected van, and entered through the back door. A small empty coffee shop consumed one side of the short hallway, but the Blue Moon barroom on the opposite side had activity with the unmistakable voice of Elton John singing *Your Song*. Each table in the barroom had a purple lava lamp illuminating the otherwise dark room with poignant lavender shadows. Black Berry smiled and waved at a couple of guys sitting at one of the tables holding hands. His first reaction was disbelief that he might find a gay bar in "Hicksville," Arizona, but it turned to delight when he realized the hotel would provide a perfect place to hide out.

At the front desk, a waiting clerk stood a foot taller than him, and weighed a hundred or so pounds more. He wore a sleeveless shirt showing dark spidery arms with a black widow tattooed on the side of each upper arm. He had fuzzy dark hair, rounded full lips, and a mustache and goatee neatly trimmed, Black Berry thought, to look like the veiled portion of a bikini waxed woman.

The clerk eyed Black Berry, starting at his boots, and slowly moving upward, briefly stopping at his crotch then finally meeting his eyes. "You need a room?" He smiled, small and coyly.

"One overlooking the street," Black Berry said.

"What happened to your face?"

"You should see the other guy."

"Oh," the clerk said and shrugged, "Makes you look . . . um . . . interesting."

"I thought it was disfiguring."

"Adds character."

"That's good," Black Berry said, "but what about the room?"

"Okay, sure . . . all our rooms have double beds and TVs with video players. We rent the videos for ten dollars a night." He fingered through file cards with movie titles stamped on them: Custer's Big Horn, Jack and Jack Back-to-Back, Long Came Tyrone, etc.

"A single room overlooking the street would be great," Black Berry said.

"Oh, are you alone?"

"Just passing through."

"I can give you a room for yourself for forty-seven bucks, or if you prefer, I can arrange company. That would cost you a hundred or so more—" the clerk shrugged again "—depending."

"Male or female?" Black Berry asked.

"Your choice." The clerk answered and smiled broadly, showing straight, clean teeth.

"Company would be nice."

The clerk continued to smile. "I'm Rocky."

"Well, Rocky, I'm Billy."

"Room one, top of the stairs, turn right, it's for *special* guests," Rocky handed over a key. "Do you want anything from the bar?"

"Whatever," Black Berry said.

"Any videos?"

"Whatever."

"It's all extra."

"I got cash," Black Berry called back and headed up the stairs, taking the steps two at a time. "And after tomorrow, I'll have a lot more."

Twenty-Three

Howard "Jiffy" McGuire owned a hound dog named Bullet. Bullet, like Jiffy, had been a prodigious mountain lion hunter in his younger days. Now, aged and arthritic, he occupied an old cotton mattress on his master's front porch. When Jiffy arrived home beleaguered, tired, and rejected after being ridiculed at the saloon, he was locked out of his own house. So he shoved Bullet aside and piled onto the mattress to share the dog's bed—and fleas.

Jiffy stared at the porch's bead board ceiling, a ceiling he'd put up years earlier simply because Gertrude didn't want to look at the bare rafters. He wanted nothing more than to sleep, but his mind raced—his life with her reeling before him. It was a marriage hindered by a fast-talking, sharp dressing Casanova from their youth, a Casanova named Tony J.C. Forkner.

In Jiffy's judgment, he did all the things he did, little and big, for a woman who gave her youth to a man he loathed. She'd always wanted that man, but settled for him, a hometown boy with no aspirations. She'd settled for someone who could never live up to her insatiable desires and demands and longings.

Things would have been so good for him if only that son of a bitch had kept his hands to himself, Jiffy thought. If only he had not touched her, kissed her lips, fondled her breasts, felt the curve of her hips, fingered her . . . if

148

only he had not planted his seed for a daughter Jiffy was expected to raise, but had failed so miserably in doing.

Trude, a name Gertrude had dreamed up by shortening her own, started a grunge, gothic rebellion against him by age ten, and by twelve she'd taken to odd streaks of color in her hair—orange, blue, green, red— and makeup Jiffy considered equally as appalling. By fifteen, she'd settled on a stark white face, orange hair; black lips, fingernails, and eye shadow; and dastardly two-inch soled black boots with straps and buckles. By eighteen she was dragging bearded, pot smoking, freeloading, hippy, gothic, grunge wannabes of any age home until, finally, Jiffy'd had enough and against Gertrude's objections sent her packing. Sometimes he missed her but not often.

Jiffy had called Trude before taking up with the dog. Hoping for what? He wasn't sure, but maybe a little understanding and comfort would have been nice.

"Hello," she'd said all innocent and pure. But he could hear the party going on, an orgy in his mind, and when he'd told her who was calling, she'd asked what he wanted, like he was an inconvenience of gigantic proportion.

"Your mother locked me out of the house and isn't home. I could use a shower and maybe a bed for a little while," he'd said as if they were family.

"No way . . . I have company."

"Anybody I know?"

"I doubt it."

"Is it J.C. Forkner? He's in town."

"Who?"

"Tony Forkner. You know, your real father."

"Go to hell, dad," she'd said and hung up.

"Maybe that's just what I'll do," he mumbled, still staring at the bead board ceiling. "Maybe that's just what I'll do,"

He was sobbing again when he heard the car pull into the driveway, and he watched through swollen eyes as Gertrude approached. Although only a year apart in age, she'd retained her youthful figure and radiant beauty and looked ten years younger than him. The years had been good to her, while devastating to him.

"Where you been?" he asked.

"To see Trude. You remember her, don't you?"

"The orange haired, black lipped monster from hell?"

"She's your daughter."

"Never was, never will be."

"Don't start again, Howard. And what are you doing out here?"

"Couldn't get in the house, so I'm sleeping out here."

"Go find a hotel, you look like hell."

"J.C.'s in town. Did you know that?"

"No kidding," she said, her reaction neutral, uncaring. In Jiffy's mind, however, her shoulders rolled back, and a faint smile touched the corners of her ruby lips.

"Yeah, your lover," he said.

"For crying out loud, Howard, we dated when we were young, kids really. Is that why you've been acting like an idiot lately because Tony's in town? What's the matter with you?"

"And you *dated* him after we were married."

"Listen to what I say for the umpteenth time: I married you. I married you because you were a rock, not some flighty pool hustler who never had a chance at anything like a solid, normal home life."

"Is that why you locked me out of the house, because you knew he was in town?"

"Howard, we've had a good life together. Think of the good times we've had, just you and me, and Trude at times—your daughter. The daughter you drove away because of your obsession over Tony. We've been over this a hundred times; there's never been any longing or dreaming of anyone else all these years."

"Then why'd you lock me out?"

"You're driving me nuts. That's why I locked you out. You won't take a bath. You won't change clothes. If you want to act and smell like the dog, you can sleep with him."

"Yeah . . . well . . . I'm going to take care of that conceited son of a bitch this time. He'll be out of my life for good."

"Is that why you're wearing a gun, like some wild west outlaw? I didn't even know you still had the old thing."

"I keep it in the work van, and I've been practicing."

"Are you going to shoot him now?"

151

Mose Duane

"As sure as shit, I am."

"You crazy old coot, you better come on inside, clean yourself up, and get some sleep. And then you can think about what you're doing before you hurt yourself." Gertrude pushed her way through the door, but left it unlocked.

Stubbornly refusing to go into the house, Jiffy stayed on the old cotton mattress staring at the bead board, scratching at his neck with one hand, and swatting at beastie flies with the other. He'd convinced himself she'd only used him until J.C. returned, and she would leave him the minute that Casanova bastard snapped his fingers. The thought of J.C. Forkner lording over him all these years had destroyed him and his life. There could be only one way to set things straight.

Twenty-Four

When Troy left Tex Bowman and the redhead to do whatever they do at the rodeo grounds, he slowly drove home. It gave him time to rehash some of the things he'd already mulled over during the flight. It didn't help because he came to the same conclusions and made the same decision.

His house, a small brick veneered structure, was solidly constructed on six wooded acres south of town on Palomino Street with a full-size front porch typical of the area and era in which it was built. He'd bought it soon after returning home from the Air Force and immediately after becoming an Upland police officer.

He unlocked the front door and walked directly into a neat and clean living-room, a room filled with matching floral imprinted couch and chair, and woodgrain coffee and end tables. Though none of it matched her rodeo lifestyle, Holly had picked it all out because she couldn't stand the "junk" he'd lived on. Before Holly, it was just a house, a place for him to eat and sleep. Now it was a home, their home. Even though she'd pretty much moved in on the very night of their first meeting, now two weeks shy of their one-year anniversary, it seemed like she'd always been there.

In the bedroom, the curtains were drawn, scented candles flickered on the nightstands, and Holly was lying on the bed on her back, drop dead gorgeous naked.

"Jesus," Troy said.

"Is that a good Jesus or a bad Jesus?"

Troy sat on the edge of the bed, trying to look at the candles. "Where'd you go?"

"Hawaii," she answered.

"What?"

"I came home, silly, to take a shower. I figured you guys ran off to the saloon or the airport, so I had lunch with Tex and the girls first, then I came home to wait for you."

"We actually stayed and watched you and Chance then I . . . well—" he didn't want to tell her that he was stupid jealous when he saw her with the cowboy "—well, I went for a short flight."

"And?"

"Good clinic," he said changing the subject. "You did great."

"Chance is a beautiful horse. Anyone riding her would do great."

"Maybe Cowboy Bob would sell her."

"I couldn't take care of a horse. Where would I keep her?"

"Well, I've been thinking," he said.

"Did you hurt yourself?"

"Holly, I want to be serious for a moment . . . and it would be easier if you put some clothes on."

She rubbed his leg. "I thought you were Mister Dildo?"

"I came in here to ask you to marry me," he blurted in frustration. It came out as if he had no control. He bit his lower lip. Here was a guy who could stare down the barrel of a shotgun without flinching, a guy who could fly an airplane upside down fifty feet above the runway without breaking a sweat. A guy who could make wonderful, intimate love to a woman he loved, but like a high school geek, couldn't control his own words when trying to tell that woman how he felt about her.

"Why would I want to do that?" Holly asked.

"Well," he rummaged for something to say, "I've got all this property here, and we could fence it in for a horse, and, well, since you're pregnant, I thought—"

"You thought you'd do the right thing?"

"Well, yes."

"Screw you, Troy."

"What?"

She jumped up and ran into the bathroom.

"Come on, Holly—" he stood up between the bathroom door and the bed "—give me a chance to finish. I've given this a lot of thought and, although I don't really know much about your history, ah, your past, umm, you know what I mean, your family and everything, well, shit Holly, I love you, and—"

The bathroom door burst open, and Holly leaped through the air. Four limbs wrapped around him and sent him staggering onto the bed with her latched on tight. "It's about time," she cried, "and I love you too."

She then began removing his clothing and they rolled on the bed until he too was naked, and stiff as a ball bat. Then, just before hitting a home run, she stopped him in mid-stroke. "Are you sure we can buy a horse?"

They laughed into a wild culmination of sharing their love.

Twenty-Five

Upland's town square was a full quarter of a mile on each of its four sides. It had been an integral part of the town since its inception but was not officially dedicated to the people of Upland until 1888 when the founding fathers thought the town was going to become the county seat. They had planned to build a massive courthouse with a clock tower dead center, surrounded by indigenous trees and a well-groomed lawn. The courthouse was never built, of course, but a twelve thousand square-foot, single span picnic building was erected in 1932. Meandering sidewalks lined with nightlights and statues were installed over the years, along with randomly strewn picnic tables and park benches, which were in constant use by locals and visitors up from the hot lowlands of Arizona.

Looking spiffy again in all new duds, J.C. and son found one of those park benches beneath an old oak tree facing the saloon. They leaned back, relaxed, and watched the quiet, methodical traffic crawl around the square. Although the seemingly intense sun blinded them intermittently, the day was cool and pleasant. The wind rustled through the trees, chirping birds scurried about, and a squirrel scampered headfirst down one oak, across the grass, and up another, with an acorn in its jaws. The day looked and smelled like early fall.

"It sure is nice here, Pop," Kid said as he slumped onto the bench, folded his hands behind his head and looked up into the trees. "I can see why you like it. But I don't understand why you left."

J.C. stretched his legs out and set fire to a bowed and rumpled cigarette. "Delusions of grandeur, kiddo, delusions of grandeur." he let out a billow of smoke. "I thought I was going to make my fortune playing pool."

"Even after you lost the saloon to Hog, you still thought you were good enough?"

"That was luck, son. A fluke, pure and simple, and I never believed, not for a moment, that it had anything to do with a lack of abilities on my part."

"What happened? I know he slopped in the nine-ball. Everyone in the world knows that by now. We've heard it like a thousand times. What I want to know is what set the game up in the first place? Why would you even consider such a thing?"

"It's not something I'm particularly proud of, but nothing I'm ashamed of either. I suppose you have a right to know and you're probably also old enough." J.C. took another long pull from his cigarette, let the smoke filter through his teeth, and forlornly looked across the street at the saloon. "Hog came in all covered in grease, I recall," J.C. continued as if he hadn't stopped, "he'd been working on some 'piece of shit motorcycle' he called it. Then after getting half lit on Seagram's or some such, he started going on about how he was a member of a cycle gang in California. How they were all fantastic pool players and how he was the best of the bunch. He was a good player, I could tell, but still sloppy, and talking so much bullshit—" J.C. shrugged "—that I arrogantly told

158

him that I'd put up the saloon against that *piece of shit motorcycle* of his on a Nine Ball session, first to five games to keep it simple. Then, when he told me he could also get his hands on a couple of grand cash to make the pot fairer, well son, 'game on,' I said never for a moment taking into consideration that I might lose, only thinking I was going to be two thousand richer and own a crap motorcycle I had no use for."

"Aren't you the one who always told me to never let your emotions get in the way of good judgment?"

"It's a good lesson learned, I guess."

"No," Kid said after he thought for a moment. "It was not arrogance or hustle that led you to such a dumb bet. No, that's not the whole story, right? You still haven't told me why, have you?"

"Son, what is it? Do you want me to confess all my sins to you right here, right now?"

"It's why you brought me out here because you wanted to talk to me. You have something on your mind, so, yes, you should tell me everything."

J.C. gave the boy a quick look over. "I know I've said this before, but are you sure you're only thirteen?"

"Thirteen and a half," Kid said proudly.

"Thirteen and a half, my blunder, and it's true given the circumstances that maybe I should tell you what drives a man to do maddening things." J.C. took another draw from the cigarette and continued. "I understand it's hard to believe looking at me now, but at one time there was a young lady in town who thought me handsome, and

I cared a great deal for her too. I was so far gone for her that I even considered marriage."

"Did you love her?"

"Ah, there it is, son, love. A four-letter word I'm sure I don't understand or even know what it means. What I am sure of, though, is that in the end, the young lady that I cared so much for asked me not to interfere in her life anymore. Said I was too 'flighty' and not stable enough to settle down and raise a family, and that it might be best if I just left town so that I couldn't be an influence in her or her impending baby's life. I confess, son, I was broken-hearted, and after that, I had no feelings one way or the other about keeping the saloon, so the wager was no big deal to me, and I wasn't devastated over losing either, not like everybody else in town seemed to be anyway. It was almost like a gift, an encumbrance lifted from my shoulders.

"Jiffy McGuire's wife, wasn't it?"

"Well son, truth is truth."

"So, I do have a sister."

"When I protested, she told me the baby wasn't mine and that I'd just be in the way if I thought otherwise. I had no reason to believe she was lying. But of course, there is always that possibility."

Kid frowned. "Does that mean we have to leave now and not buy the saloon, because of something you did a hundred years ago?"

"A hundred years? The way I feel sometimes, it seems that might be right. But no, all that's history, an uncontrolled past, a fork in the road not taken. No,

Trude's an adult now, someone I don't even know, someone who will be raising her own family soon, I would suppose. Therefore, I don't feel obligated to leave town again because of that."

"So, we can buy it?"

"Well, now to the point of why we're out here, son. I've been thinking, if we use the cash we have on hand, everyone will start asking questions about where we got it. Questions we won't be able to answer, and, I must admit, it's something I didn't consider in the heat of the moment back when I lit that damn fuse."

"Why is it I get the headache when *you've* been thinking? So now we're back to not buying it."

J.C. raised his eyebrows and smiled. "So, son, what I've been thinking is that there might be a better way."

"What better way?"

"Hog offered to play me for the ring as down payment for the saloon, right?"

"That's your better way. Next to your Rambow, the ring's your greatest possession, and the way you're shooting—"

"But here's the God's truth, son." J.C. field-stripped his cigarette butt and let the tobacco spread with a gust of wind, then fired up another. "You're my greatest possession and . . . well, I don't suppose I own you, but you get my drift. Anyway, I think I've wasted all my talent on booze and tobacco and such, so I don't think I still have the ability it'll take to beat Hog."

"I love you too, Dad," Kid said and smiled. "So now, we're back to buying it, with no money."

"Not necessarily. Like I said, there may be a better way."

"That's what you said." Kid shook his head.

"And it could be a way to get your mother—the real true love of my life—to come back to us. It'll give her a home of sorts, a place to stay and take care of you."

"I'd like that."

"So would I, son, so would I. And here it is, with just a little bit of luck, kiddo, I think *you* could beat Hog."

"Me?" Kid sprang to his feet and looked at his father, "Sure maybe for ten or twenty bucks, but not for thousands, not for your ring, not for the saloon."

"Settle down. A game is a game. Whether it's for a dollar, a thousand, or ten thousand, it's still the same game. The best way to overcome the added pressure is to just put it in your head that you're playing for ten dollars and play your best."

"But it's not ten dollars and I know it." Kid eased back onto the bench.

"We've been over this before, son. By controlling your emotions, you'll control the pressure. It's what separates the balls from the pussies. If you have the balls, you'll be able to play for ten or ten thousand and it won't affect your abilities. If you're a pussy, you'll be beaten playing for beers."

"Well, I think I've got . . . I think I'm man enough."

"Okay, that's what I wanted to hear. Now, look at it this way to ease your mind somewhat. If you win, we are home free. If, however, you happen to lose or if Hog gets lucky again, then we'll ponder the outcome of buying it with Troy's help or making payments to Hog. Neither option is anything I want to do, but if that's what it takes—" J.C. shrugged "—then that's what we'll do. How's that sound?"

"If I lose, I'll lose your ring."

"It's only a ring, worth a couple of grand at most and only if you could find some crazy bastard crazy enough to buy it."

"Hog would buy it."

"There's my point, son. Hog's crazy enough to stake the saloon for it."

Kid considered the idea for a moment, and then smiled. "As crazy as you were a hundred years ago?"

"Humph. Now that hurts, son. That hurts."

"It would have to be Nine Ball."

"I agree."

"And we have to fix the table."

"I think we can con Hog into doing both."

"And I want a new set of balls."

"Balls?"

"Aramith Pros . . . with a red dot cue-ball and a shark eight-ball."

"Now you're trying to rob me," J.C. said, leaned back on the bench, set fire to the last cigarette in the pack, blew a chain of small smoke rings, and smiled.

Twenty-Six

In the hotel room, Black Berry did not bother locking the door. Normally, he would leave nothing to chance when it came to prostitutes, male or female. He would not only secure the door but would also check to ensure there were no other entrances, secret doors, passages, or such, through which some snake—much like himself—could slither in and out unnoticed. He'd engineered just such a scheme in a sleazy hotel in Vegas only a year or two back. There was a connecting door to the adjacent room where he could slip in and then out with a substantial prize while a prostitute of one persuasion or another kept the occupant especially busy. He'd managed to supplement his and the prostitute's daily take with stealthy ease and skill. That was in Vegas, however, not the high country of Arizona, and he was sure any company he got here would be wanted, or at least easy to control.

He removed his 45 and wedged it behind his pillow between the mattress and the headboard. That would be his only precaution tonight. He emptied his pockets—keys, wallet, some change, and placed them on the bureau. He removed the sheet of acid from his vest, unfolded it, tore off a tab, and carefully placed it on his tongue.

Sitting on the bed with his hands folded in his lap, he waited for the impending high to take him on its long assent. Up, up, and away, he thought and visualized a hot

165

air balloon on a relaxing, pleasurable, air skimming slide upward, taking him from firm reality to the intricate, but gratifying, world of euphoric dreams, floating ever so steadily up into a world that had become more and more satisfying each time he partook in the American elite's candy of preference.

Thinking of pleasures had, and those to be had, he impatiently tore off another tab and placed it on the other side of his tongue. He then stood and slowly undressed in front of the bureau mirror, teasing himself as a stripper might, swaying to a beat only he could hear, and becoming aroused while admiring his own small, but muscular frame.

He neatly folded his clothing over the nightstand and felt more pride than awkwardness padding to the bathroom naked. As he took a relaxing shower, along with thoughts of stopping J.C.'s heart with a single bullet hole, he anticipated large, shaggy arms and hands rubbing his inner thighs with gentle, kneading fingers.

Back in the bedroom, standing in front of the window toweling off, he hoped to see J.C. walking in or out of one of the saloons at the far side of the town square. However, blocking his view were large, mesmerizing trees, their tops swaying in the wind, back and forth, back and forth, and around and around in great fascinating, mind bending green and silver swirls, lighted by bright streetlights and colorful neon signs. His head followed the sway like the random movements of a turbulent sea— up, down, round and round. The swirling, ebbing winds whistled through his brain until he staggered backwards and fell onto the bed. The room rolled, tossing him to-and-fro, as if he were a ship in that turbulent sea, up, up high on the crest of a wave, and then down, deep down to the bottom of the trough, his mast ever so skyward. "Whee," he called in a low voice, like an eight-year-old recalling wild childhood innertube rides down the Ohio River, "whee, whee, whee." He grabbed fistfuls of bed covers and hung on in delight.

Then, as the room settled and his attention became single minded, he watched a spider scurry diagonally across the ceiling, all eight furry legs in focus and moving in sensual harmony, and he marveled at the idea of fornicating with the spider. He chuckled at the strange word. "Fornicate," he said and continued to chuckle as he drifted deeper into the nether lands of his mind. "Fornicate," he told the spider as its red head appeared above him.

"Fornicate," a redheaded spider said and laughed.

Twenty-Seven

"**Do** you believe in miracles?"

J.C. and Kid were still on the park bench enjoying the afternoon while discussing their strategy for playing Hog. When J.C. heard someone else speaking, he looked up into the sun, shaded his eyes with his hand, and saw Jiffy McGuire standing a couple of yards away.

"What was that partner?" J.C. asked.

"I said do you believe in miracles?" Jiffy's voice trembled.

J.C. squinted into the low evening sun to focus on his newest nemesis.

"Because it'd be a frigging miracle if I missed you from here." Jiffy was standing, feet spread slightly, his wrinkled hand hovering over a revolver holstered low on his right hip. Black baggy circles ringed bloodshot eyes that glared from a pasty face with quivering, pallid lips. His house-painting garb looked as if he'd been in them for a week.

"Christ," J.C. said. "Christ O Mighty. You don't look too good, partner."

"I haven't slept for two or three days, not since you been here."

"Well, there you go, that ain't healthy."

"And don't you call me partner. It sounds like an insult coming from you."

"Yeah, well, okay, but seems to me if you're so hell-bent on shooting me, why do it right here in front of my boy? I know you don't have any big old grudge against him just because he took you for few bucks on the pool table, so why does he have to watch?"

"Gertrude locked me out of the house," Jiffy said, his gaze not averting from J.C.

J.C. elbowed Kid, who looked dumbstruck. "High tail it across the street, kiddo, and give Troy a holler." Then to Jiffy he said, "You don't mind if he calls Troy?"

"I went home, and she had the locks changed," Jiffy said, "and she threw my stuff out on the porch, and Trude wouldn't take me in, so I've been trying to sleep with my dog."

J.C. elbowed Kid again, "Go on son," he said and took a long pull on his cigarette while Kid eased off the bench. J.C. made three smoke rings as if nothing of importance was happening and watched Kid hustle between cars to cross the street as quickly as possible. He then turned his attention back to Jiffy. "Now, partner, how is it my fault that she locked you out and your daughter rejected you? I didn't go see either of them or anything like that."

Jiffy's eyes were fixed. "It was from the start. You ruined my marriage from the start. You and your good looks and smooth ways and fancy talking, you screwed with her mind. You got her pregnant and then left town."

A small crowd was starting to gather.

"Okay, I always prided myself in my appearance. But was it my fault women took to me?"

"Like Gertrude, maybe," someone in the background said and snickered. Others joined in.

"Now you guys don't go egging him on. He has a valid point here," J.C. said to no one in particular.

"Like Gertrude," Jiffy looked at the crowd. "Me and him—" he pointed a shaky finger toward J.C. "—were friends, best friends, and he . . . he had to go and fill her head with dreams and lies . . . promised her all sorts of things just to get in her panties, and—"

"Times gone by," J.C. said, "the past, water under the bridge. It's history, partner, a thing you learn from, not a thing you live in."

"That's it. You're full of crap, you talk crap, all the time talking, all the time analyzing, all the time explaining, you think everyone else is so damn dumb. You're so full of crap."

"I'm full of crap, partner, I know it, you know it, hell the whole town knows it, but it's no reason to draw on me."

Someone in the crowd let out a robust laugh. The throng of onlookers had grown exponentially, milling around and amused, nothing seemed serious.

"It's all a joke to you. Things have no meaning to you, except for screwing maybe, and drinking, and shooting pool maybe, but that's all."

"Apart from the order, perhaps, you got me. I'm one superficial bastard, I know, I admit it. But that's still no good reason to go and shoot me."

"So, was she a good screw?"

"What?" J.C. was stunned.

Some in the crowd snickered.

"I need to know." Jiffy said. "Was she a good lay for you?"

"She's your wife for Christ's sake. She's the mother of your daughter," J.C. said knowing that's what Gertrude had always wanted him to say, but not so sure he was telling the truth. "There's no need to speak about her like that."

"She's the mother of *your* daughter that I raised."

"I'm not sure that's at all a true statement, Jiffy. But even if it were, it's no reason to gun me down."

More snickering from the crowd.

"I once had a girl over in Prescott when we were kids, sucked my knob," Jiffy said, eyes welling. "But I never screwed her."

J.C. bolted upright and took a long drag of the cigarette. "Now that's funny stuff, Jiffy, but not hardly appropriate."

"Right there in the living room of her house while her parents were at church."

J.C. chuckled and the crowd followed suit. "At church, huh?"

"She was the only other girl I knew in that way."

"Christ, Jiffy, don't make me laugh," J.C. said. "It hurts my side."

"So, was she a good piece of ass? I got no one to compare her to, not like you, you who's screwed hundreds—"

"I'm not sure hundreds is right," J.C. said, "hell, that'd have me being with every female in town."

The horde hooted, hollered, and made catcalls.

"Then she was just one of many, nothing special?" Jiffy asked.

"No, that's not what I remember. I remember her being very special. Long, lean, clean, and smelled good too, I remember. Like lilac or something."

"That's supposed to make me feel better." Jiffy's face turned red. "Well, it doesn't."

"Settle down, Jiffy," someone in the crowd said, "you can't blame him. You've always had trouble with your daughter, and you and Gertrude have been having marital problems for years."

"Just the thought of him with her ruined my marriage. He put a thirty-year cloud over my bedroom."

"Jesus Christ, Jiffy, it was only a fling . . . or two, nothing serious," J.C. said. "She chose you over me; you should have been content to be with her and the girl for all these years."

"Stand up," Jiffy said. "I'm going to do what I should have done years ago."

"What's that, partner?" J.C. asked as he stood to face the ghostly man. His now stub of a cigarette had moved to the side of his mouth.

Some in the crowd stood silent, others continued to chuckle and point at the hilarity of the two men, one dressed fresh and flawless, and the other messy and foul and standing like a Wild West caricature.

"I'm going to put six rounds in you before you hit the ground from the first one," Jiffy said.

"Now, wait a minute. Aren't you the quick draw expert? How would it be fair if you just shot me right here in front of God and everybody? Wouldn't you feel better if I could defend myself and you could prove you could outdraw me?" J.C. held his right hand to his side, fingers curled, ready to draw a gun he didn't have.

The crowd roared. "Come on Jiffy, give him a chance," someone from the back shouted.

"Yeah, let's see a fair gunfight," another yelled.

"Give him a gun," still another offered, "are you afraid he's faster than you?"

Sirens overtook the crowd's spirited laughter and Jiffy blankly scanned them with glazed eyes. "I'll show you," he said. "I'll show all of you, you sons of bitches," and lightning fast he drew his revolver and pointed it at J.C. but did not fire. "I'll show all of you." He twirled the revolver once, holstered it, spun on one foot, and swiftly walked away.

J.C. slumped back onto the bench, hands clutching his chest trying to contain his wildly pounding heart. "Damn, I thought that was it," he said fumbling for another cigarette, but finding only an empty pack.

"Jesus Christ," Hog said to J.C. as he busted through the crowd carrying a sawed-off pool cue that he kept behind the bar for protection. "I thought you were dead meat."

J.C. wadded the empty cigarette pack into a ball and threw it at a nearby trashcan. It glanced off the rim. "I am," he said. "Closer than you think."

"Okay, where's the trouble?" A black female police officer also broke through the pack. She looked like a professional model, tall and thin and striking, her uniform fit like the latest runway fashion. Troy, wearing a rumpled uniform, no hat, hair a mess, quickly followed her.

"No trouble," J.C. said, "just a little confusion, a misunderstanding, I think."

"Someone reported a gunfight," the female officer said.

"Didn't happen!" came from the crowd.

"J.C.?" Troy's voice was stern.

"It was Jiffy, he's drunk and packing."

"Jiffy?" the officer questioned. She was young enough not to know many old timers, and certainly not their nicknames.

"Howard McGuire is his real name," Troy told her. "He's probably headed home to sleep it off." Troy then introduced her to J.C. Her name was Nina Miller and she'd been on the force for three years. After the introductions, she hung around just long enough for Troy to promise her that he would swing by the station later to make a full report.

"Where's Kid?" J.C. asked Hog as he watched Nina disappear into the crowd.

"He's across the street. I made him stay put."

J.C. then looked at Troy and grinned. "I must say, brother, you look like shit."

Troy grinned. "I think I'm getting married."

"Come on," J.C. waved to the crowd, "drinks are on me."

Twenty-Eight

Hog and Dana poured liquor as if it were iced tea at a picnic, and once everyone had received at least one free drink, the charging began and the cash register rang "like sweet Christmas bells," J.C. said.

Some patrons lifted their drinks to J.C. and Troy, downed them in one gulp, smiled and headed back across the street. Regulars found seats or milled about. Most, passing J.C. and Troy slapping them on the back, telling J.C. how lucky he was, how brave he was, how crazy he was, how he hadn't heard the last of Jiffy, how he'd never see Jiffy again, how Troy should go and arrest Jiffy right now. All also congratulated Troy on his upcoming nuptials, though most had never doubted it was going to happen.

"I think the whole town got wind of your generosity," Hog said to J.C. over the ruckus.

"Good for business, Hog. You should do this more often."

"What? Have Jiffy shoot you or have Troy get married?"

J.C. raised his glass. "He only threatened; and this is going to be Troy's only wedding."

Troy, still on duty, raised his glass of Pepsi to return his brother's toast. "We've both been blessed."

"Blessed is what I'd call it," Hog said, "and maybe it's time to think about buying me out. Look how much money you could make. And—" he looked at Dana and smiled "—we need to get out of here."

"Okay Hog," J.C. said, "let's talk turkey."

"Ten thousand and the ring," Hog said with no apparent perceived thought.

J.C. rapped a new pack of cigarettes on the bar, possibly to pack the tobacco; he wasn't sure, but he'd done it too many years to worry about it now. He placed the unopened pack in his shirt pocket and picked up his drink. "Let's go find someplace less rowdy." Then, with Troy and Hog following, he shuffled to the pool table room.

Kid was by himself running balls. "I can't get past fifty," he said as his dad walked in.

"Nothing to brag about, son."

"You guys going to play?" Kid asked as he started to unscrew the Rambow.

"Just talking, kiddo, and this may concern you, so don't leave."

"Ten thousand and the ring," Hog repeated his proposal and shrugged.

"You're not getting the ring," J.C. said. "It has sentimental value. You know, I'm going to give it to my boy here, someday." He looked at Kid and winked then knocked back his Wild Turkey and sat the glass on the ledge. "Someday it'll be his inheritance."

"Maybe sooner than you hoped for, if you keep downing hard liquor like that." Troy said.

"Hell, this is the weak stuff. Hog knows that. He wouldn't serve hundred-proof if his life depended on it."

"Okay," Hog said, "twenty thousand without the ring, or I'll give you a chance to win it back . . . this place against the ring and maybe some money."

"Don't be crazy," Troy said. "I thought we were past all of that."

"Hey, I've been livin' upstairs for fifteen years; I didn't pay much for it in the first place, as you well know. Besides, if you get right down to it, the ring's probably worth as much as the saloon anyway."

"Could be more," J.C. said as he pulled the pack of smokes from his pocket, fussed over opening it while making sure the ring was tantalizingly visible, and then whacked the pack on a side rail of the pool table to extract a fresh cigarette. "Twenty grand easy . . . seems like that's what the guy I won it from said it was worth."

Kid frowned at his dad but said nothing.

"I think we should leave the ring and pool game out of it and just come up with the money," Troy said.

"Tell you what, Hog," J.C. ignored his brother. "Since it's going to be the boy's ring sooner or later anyway, and probably sooner like my pessimistic brother said, let's let him play you for it."

"Play the kid!" Stunned, Hog looked at Kid, then back toward J.C., and then laughed as if he'd heard a joke. "You idiots look serious . . . you're not kiddin'?"

"I thought it a good gesture on our part," J.C. said.

"I'm not sure that'd be fair," Hog said.

"Fair? What about legal?" Troy's voice pierced the room.

"I know it won't be fair," J.C. said and smiled, "but he'll not spot you anything."

"Ha-ha," Hog answered, "and I won't spot him anything either, that's for damn sure. So, we're talkin' straight up, me against the kid . . . for the ring?"

"For the saloon," J.C. said, "whichever way you care to look at it."

"Yeah, right, the ring and the saloon," Hog said and grinned, "one of us will own both when this is over."

"Christ O Mighty, Hog," J.C. said. "That's how it works."

"Are you idiots listening to me?" Troy asked. "This cannot be legal."

"What's the game?" Hog asked.

"Kid prefers Eight Ball or Straight Pool," J.C. said.

Hog considered it for a moment. "Yeah, sure, but here's the thing: I won it from you playin' Nine Ball. I think that would be fair enough. One game, winner takes all."

J.C. looked at Kid and winked again. "Nine Ball, huh? What do you think kiddo?"

"Sure, I guess." Kid shrugged and smiled.

"All right then," J.C. rolled a ball across the table and watched the slow bounce. "Nine Ball it is, but anyone can get lucky or unlucky in one game."

"Okay," Hog agreed, "we'll play first to six or seven games."

"First to seven then," Kid said, "that way there's no tie . . . and BCA rules, no house rules."

"You too," Troy looked at the boy. "You're just like your old man."

"So I've been told," Kid said smiling.

Hog looked at Kid. "Hell boy, I don't even know what BCA means, let alone knowin' all their rules."

"I know the rules."

"I'll bet."

"Okay then," J.C. summed up the wager. "It'll be a race to seven and BCA rules."

"I'm going home," Troy said and headed for the door. "If anyone gets shot, leave me out of it."

"Referee?" J.C. asked Hog.

"Like Troy said, this could be illegal as hell," Hog answered. "I don't think we need any outsiders, and we damn sure don't need no damn referees. We didn't need one last time and no one reneged, and we ain't gonna renege on this one."

"What about the pool table?" Kid asked.

Hog looked at him. "What about it?"

"Are we going to get it fixed?"

"Seems it would only be fair," J.C. said.

Hog shrugged in agreement.

"And new balls?" Kid asked.

"What's wrong with the ones we have?"

"They're old and out of round."

"Okay, okay, whatever." Hog held up his hands in submission.

Twenty-Nine

Again, Black Berry was surprised at how focused and sharp his brain could be after a night of high-quality acid bingeing, as clear and pure and uncluttered as a Sunday school teacher's mind, as long as he didn't mix it with the likes of whiskey or rum or tequila. Today was no exception, and when he opened his eyes, his mind was unencumbered, though other parts of his anatomy felt overused and abused.

"You had quite a time last night," a voice was loud and lucid.

Black Berry rolled onto his side and recalled some of the events of the past night as he recognized Rocky, who was rocking his chair back on two legs at the small round table between the bureau and the window. Across the table from Rocky, in the chair directly in the corner, a lanky, red-haired individual fumbled through Black Berry's wallet. Like Rocky, he wore a sleeveless shirt exposing a tattoo of a black widow on his upper arm. An empty bottle of Jack Daniel's and a stack of videos were neatly arranged in the middle of the table. Daylight pierced the edges of the now tightly drawn curtains. Black Berry forced a smile. "What time is it?"

"Six a-m." Rocky answered and then added, "I thought you had money?"

Black Berry lowered his eyes and watched the two men carefully while thinking about how close he was to finding J.C. and the cash. And if he could avoid it, he didn't want a confrontation with these two weirdoes. He simply wanted to do what he came for and be on his way.

"You said to bring whatever I wanted, that you had money, so I brought Joey—" he pointed toward the lanky redhead "—and some whiskey and videos."

"Videos? Black Berry questioned. "Who the hell watched videos?"

"Don't matter if you watch them or not." Joey answered in an irritating, high pitched sound. "The fact that we brought them up here is what matters."

"And the whiskey?" Black Berry kept his eyes on the skinny redhead.

"We all drank it," Rocky answered. "You were probably too far gone to remember."

"Look," Black Berry said, "I'm on my way to set some things straight with some has-been, collect some money he owes me, and will soon thereafter be on my way to Canada, so I'm in no mood for a quarrel with you two idiots. I have—or had—six or seven hundred in my wallet. That should be more than enough to pay for whatever it was we did last night."

Joey turned the wallet upside down. "Not in here." His irksome voice penetrated the room.

"This isn't turning out the way I'd hoped," Black Berry said, his forced smile turned into a more natural grimace. "If you guys are trying to screw me, it's not a good idea."

"We did that already," Rocky answered smiling at Joey. "We *fornicated*."

Joey laughed. "Yeah, we *fornicated* and now we want *paid*."

"That's all the money I had," Black Berry said. "If you took it, you've been paid. If you didn't, you're shit out of luck."

"No sir, Mister Berry," Joey said as he flipped Black Berry's driver's license in his fingers. "We're not the ones out of luck, shit or otherwise."

"Maybe we can make a deal on the fake Porsche parked out back," Rocky added.

"So, you want my money and my car . . . because you're such studs, I suppose? Where does that leave me? I mean, what do you propose doing with me?"

"Did you ever hear of rolling a queer?" Joey said and laughed. "That's all we're doing, the hundred-year-old tradition of rolling a queer, so you—you're the queer by the way—so you sign the phony Porsche over to us and you're free to go."

"You can take a one-way boat to hell," Black Berry responded, simply and calmly.

Joey spring to his feet filling the corner of the room with his tall, thin, reddish form, his limp wristed hands waving a very small pink pistol, his smirk was gone.

"You've got to be shitting me?" Black Berry said and laughed. "Everybody's got a bullshit pistol these days. What are you going to do with that pissy thing?" He eased his hand beneath his pillow.

"I'm going to shoot your faggot ass right here if you screw with me anymore," Joey screeched.

Black Berry grasped the grip of his own pistol. "You better hurry—" he turned and fired "—you redheaded freak."

Joey fell back into his seat, a .45 caliber hole in the middle of his heart.

"Fuck!" Rocky shrieked and held up his arms, hands forward, and then began to sob. "Hey man, he took your money. I had nothing to do with it . . . and the pistol, it was his idea not mine."

Black Berry spun out of bed. "Did you see that?" he said giddily. "Now that was one hell of a shot."

Rocky sat with his hands forward, sobbing. "The whole thing was Joey's idea," he said. "I liked you, man. I thought we had a good time."

"You calling me a faggot too?"

"N-no sir. Joey's the queer, a-a freak like you said. He's the faggot."

Black Berry kept an eye and his 45 trained on Rocky as he dressed. "How many people in the hotel?"

"Just a couple of foreigners," Rocky answered sniffling. "They're checked in at the other end of the hallway."

"Cleaning crew?"

"No . . . no, Joey and I did all that ourselves."

"Do you think anyone heard the shot?"

"I'm sure they've already called the cops." Rocky answered looking like he'd found new hope.

"In that case get my money," Black Berry said, "and let's get the hell out of here."

Rocky reached toward the redhead's body then pulled back. "I can't." He started to sob again. "He's got the money, but I just can't touch him, not like this."

"Goddamn it!" Black Berry leveled his pistol. "If you want to walk out of here, do as I say."

Rocky held up his hands again, tried to stifle tears and runny nose. He quickly fumbled through the dead man's pockets, retrieved a small wad of bills, and handed it to Black Berry.

"And my stuff."

Rocky pulled the folded sheet of acid from his own pocket. "You used some and Joey and I each had a tab—" he wiped tears from his cheeks "—but most of it's still here."

"Pick the freak show up and lead me out the back way to my car," Black Berry said.

Rocky looked at him. "I . . . I can't man." He began to bawl.

"Shut the fuck up! Everything was going fine for me until you two weirdos tried to rob me. I probably shouldn't have shot the asshole, but he did have a gun, didn't he? So now, we have to deal with it. But you, you got lucky because if I shoot you too then I'd have two bodies to dispose of, wouldn't I? It's something I don't normally worry about, but I can't have the cops screwing around just yet, okay?"

Rocky nodded.

"So, if you do what I say, I won't hurt you and we can even be buddies. Wouldn't you like that? And to show you that I want to be your buddy, you can keep his pistol, how's that?"

Rocky nodded again.

"Now pick the freak up and let's go."

He picked up a napkin, wiped his face, then retrieved the diminutive pink pistol, and cautiously slid it into his pants pocket. Then he easily heaved his scrawny buddy's body over his shoulder, and with blood dripping down his back soaking his shirt he hurried out of the room, down the service stairs, and out the back door to the once highly polished Porsche.

Black Berry reached inside the car, pulled a lever and the front popped open. "Throw him in there, and you drive."

Rocky stuffed the dead man into the small space and forced the lid shut. "Drive to where?" he asked. His voice cracked but the sobbing had stopped.

"The boonies, a river, a lake, somewhere where we can dump the body. Wherever you were going to dump me."

He wiped his nose on his bare arm. "Then what?"

"Then we trade IDs, and you drive the car back to town alone, and I'll walk."

"Is the car hot?"

"Shit, man! Of course it's hot. Half the cops in two states are probably looking for it, but that's the idea. If the police stop you, it'll confuse them for a while, until they clear you of any wrongdoing, and that will buy me the time I need to take care of things."

"But I'll get blood all over the car's seat," Rocky complained.

"Goddamn it, don't worry about it."

Rocky squeezed into the small car, blood squishing between him and the seat. The small pistol jabbed his leg. He quickly and slyly glanced down at it, and then at Black Berry, who seemed preoccupied. Rocky started the Porsche and drove out of town, his crying now under control.

Thirty

Upland's police department was housed in a temporary modular building underpinned with concrete blocks and had been sitting at the rear of a weedy gravel parking lot for some twenty years. The number of personnel slotted for the department was twelve total, but since most of the young inhabitants of Upland bailed out of town as soon as they graduated from high school, and few other qualified residents had any interest in being a small-town cop, there were only eight officers currently on active duty. Troy, who was still the unofficial acting chief, and the seven others had to split the week of day and night shifts as evenly and as fairly as possible. That usually meant only four officers loosely working each eight-hour shift. If events called for a larger force, they'd simply triple up and work longer shifts.

"Are you ready for the big pool game?" Nina asked as Troy walked into the station to join her on the morning schedule. Officer Nina Miller was the only daughter of one of the two African American families who lived in Upland, and the only offspring of those families to stay in town. She and Troy had dated only two years back until she called it off—reason unknown and never explained. Though Troy had said he understood and never pressed her, it had wounded him deeply. Still, like Beth, they had remained friends and excellent working companions.

"The town has flat gone nuts," Troy answered. "We may get more crazies for this stupid pool game than we'll get for the rodeo next week."

"It may be even crazier than you think," Nina said. "Think about this: your brother shows up in town with a thirteen-year-old son you never knew he had. Then Howard McGuire goes batty and starts wearing a gun— Wyatt Earp like—and threatens to shoot your brother. I drove by McGuire's house this morning and he's been sleeping on the front porch with his flea-riddled hound and says it's your brother's fault. Then, even earlier this morning, I got an anonymous phone call from some stranger who said a shot had been fired at the Grande Hotel. I drove by there too, and the place was locked up tighter than a tomb. And now this," she handed Troy a bulletin that had come in by fax sometime in the middle of the night.

Troy scanned the bulletin:

> *Be on the lookout for one Levi Berry (AKA: Black Berry), age 32. He is wanted in Los Angeles, California for questioning in connection to a robbery and homicide. He is believed to be armed and dangerous and may be headed for the Upland, Arizona area. He often passes for African American, Hispanic, or Caucasian.*

A description of Levi Berry and his automobile was also given, and normally Troy wouldn't have taken much notice of such a bulletin had two things not caught his eye. During the ruckus between his brother and McGuire, he'd noticed an illegally parked Porsche with California license plates matching the description of the car in the bulletin. On top of that, the reported robbery and homicide had taken place in geographical proximity to where J.C. had worked and lived for the past five or six years and occurred only a few days before he and his son showed up in Upland, with new duds and a new attitude.

"This could get ugly," Troy said. "I really thought I could handle the pool game on my own, and from a distance. But now, I think there's a distinct possibility there's more going on in my brother's life than he's letting on."

"You know you have my support. I'll be here if you need me."

"Thanks, but I've decided to be inside the saloon during the game."

"I'd stay clear if I were you. We both know the game is going to be illegal, to say the least."

"Yeah, that's what I said. Though they have cooked up some deal where if Kid loses, Hog will buy the ring for several thousand dollars, and if Hog loses, J.C. will buy the saloon for the same unspecified amount, to make it at least appear legal. If someone wants to sue, let a judge settle it. In the meantime, get Duke or Joe to come in and cover for you. I need you to patrol the streets, keep an eye out for a Porsche, and this guy, Berry. And be careful."

"You got it."

"And keep in radio contact at all times."

"Can do," Nina said, and Troy knew he could count on her.

He left the police station and drove past the saloon. As expected, it was filling up fast in anticipation of the big game. Among the patrons of Saloon Row, the legend of the original game between Hog and J.C. had grown disproportional to its importance, and very few had even witnessed it. To those people, today's game seemed to be equally as important, and Troy understood none would want to miss it.

He didn't stop at the saloon, but drove home to get Holly, who had volunteered to help Dana tend bar during the game.

"I'm ready to go," Holly shouted from the bedroom as Troy walked into the house.

"Things have changed," Troy hollered back. "It could get rowdy down there, and it would make me feel better if you stayed home today."

"Rowdier than usual?" Holly asked as she walked into the room to greet him, her denim shirt hanging unbuttoned and loose on her shoulders showing her propensity for going braless, and her tight jeans displaced little body fat around her waist. Her dark hair framed a clear, flawless face, and cascaded down her shoulders.

"Yeah, maybe even dangerous . . . God, Holly, you'll just make it worse looking like that. You'll have every guy in there trying to pat your ass."

"Ooo, sounds exciting." She wrapped her arms around him and gave him a passionate kiss. "Are you worried or jealous?"

"Maybe I'm just worried about the baby—" Troy broke away from her "—we wouldn't want *him* to get hurt."

"*She'll* be okay," Holly said, "and besides, I expect everyone to support me at the rodeo next week, so I'm going to be there to help my new sponsors in their time of need."

"Fine," Troy said holding up his hands. "But if anything happens—"

"Is worry all you do?" She grabbed his hand and pulled him out the door.

"At least finish dressing," he told her as they climbed into the patrol car.

They cruised around the town square as much as the morning turtle-paced traffic allowed. People already wandering about the saloons, crossing the street helter-skelter while illegally carrying drinks, didn't help Troy's nagging gut feeling that something disastrous was inevitable. However, he saw nothing that looked overly dangerous or suspicious and certainly no Porsche.

They passed Nina driving in the opposite direction and Troy keyed his radio twice. She smiled and waved.

"She's as cute as ever," Holly said.

"Are you worried or jealous?"

Holly dug her fingernails into his inner thigh. "I'm crazy jealous. I'll always be crazy jealous when you smile at pretty girls."

Troy laughed. "This'll be good. A crazy jealous couple gets married and has a house full of crazy kids."

"We'll fit right in here in Upland," she said pointing to the circus gathering around Saloon Row.

"You're right. Even people who normally couldn't care less about a pool game are showing up to see what's going on."

He parked the patrol car in a no parking zone on Rawhide Street at the side of the Last Chance, and, with Holly on his heels, he pushed his way into the pending chaos.

Thirty-One

Over two hundred years earlier, luckless gold miners, silver miners, and copper miners, finding nothing more valuable than onyx, quartz, and pyrite, settled Upland. Sometime around the turn of the century while most small towns were building tall, iron water towers, the miners, all being experts in pushing dirt and boulders from one place to another, built an earthen dam at the mouth of two mountain streams. The dam created a large reservoir three miles in distance and a thousand feet in elevation above the town for a dependable water supply. Given the frequent rains and abundant snowfalls, it never ran dry.

A dirt road started on the east side of town, snaked in switchback fashion up to the dam, crossed it, and twisted back down to reenter the town on the west side. After a harrowing twenty-minute ride, after Black Berry had twice told Rocky to slow down or risk getting his head blown off, they parked at the edge of the dam, in front of a small, gradual boat ramp.

Black Berry looked the area over carefully. It was now full daylight, but a slight mist of fog drifting across the water along with dense foliage of small trees and shrubs provided ample cover. The only sound was a coyote's howl from some distance away, and he could see two campsites across the reservoir. But no fishing boats were on the lake yet, and no one was fishing along the banks yet either. "Pull down the ramp," he ordered.

194

"What the hell?" Rocky questioned. "Can't we just put him into the water?" He began to sob again.

"Shit." Black Berry waved the 45, "just do what I say before someone shows up."

Wiping tears, Rocky started to protest but his eyes locked onto the pistol bulging in his pocket. The interior of the car was relatively dark.

"Look, it'll be easier to unload the body," Black Berry calmly explained. He was intently scanning the lake for boats or anglers.

Rocky shook his head as if he understood, wiped his eyes, and carefully drove down the ramp. He stopped when the front bumper touched water.

"A little further," Black Berry said and shoved the 45 into Rocky's ribs.

"If we go much farther, we won't get out," Rocky complained as he carefully began sliding his hand into his pocket.

"The engine and drive train are in the rear. We'll get out."

Halfway into the water Rocky stopped again. "Come on, man," he said, again fighting back tears as his hand grasped the pistol handle. "We're starting to float."

"Yeah, maybe you're right." Black Berry grabbed Rocky's arm before the small pistol cleared his pocket and squeezed the trigger of his 45 at the same time. He hoped the slug had pierced Rocky's heart. Not that it mattered much, he simply liked the idea of stopping the human machinery with a single bullet, and the heart, of course, was his favorite target. The blast erupted within the confines of the small automobile but from across the lake, he doubted it would sound much louder than the diminutive pistol Rocky was gripping as he slumped onto the steering wheel.

The car began slipping further into the water and Black Berry slid out leaving his door slightly ajar. He then gave his prized Porsche one small shove. It floated out and away from the ramp. With the weight evenly distributed between bodies and engine, it kept a reasonably even keel, just a slight listing to the left, until it finally filled with water and made its journey to the bottom of the reservoir.

Black Berry's concern wasn't necessarily dumping the bodies. He could have simply left them in the hotel room. Years ago, on his first job, he'd spent four grueling hours in the hot Nevada desert burying two stiffs from Jersey, and swore he'd never again worry over the disposal of his handiwork. It was clearly not in his job description, as far as he was concerned. His beloved Porsche, on the other hand, had to be discarded, and since it was a package deal, why not feed the fish?

Thirty-Two

Except for a century's worth of cigarette burns on the oak top rails and the cracking laminate peeling from the cabinet and legs, the old King pool table could have been a new one. It was now flat and level with a handsome green covering of a tightly woven blend of wool and nylon, with a fluffy nap. Fearing a slight loss of cue-ball control, neither Hog nor Kid liked to shoot on slick, napless cloth. New cushion rubber responded to the slightest touch of the new highly polished Aramith balls, and fresh leather pockets prevented rim shots and kick outs of a well struck ball.

Kid and Hog lagged for choice of the first break. Kid put a perfect roll on the gleaming new shark eight-ball, and easily won. He selected to go first. They agreed that the loser of any game thereafter would perform subsequent breaks and the winner would rack the balls, eliminating the possibility of one player dominating the table.

Hog racked the balls in a tight diamond shape with the one-ball at the head, the nine-ball in the center and the remaining in a seemingly random fashion.

Kid broke with the ferociousness of someone twice his size. The balls scattered, the eight-ball fell, but the one-ball stayed at the far end of the table leaving a hindered shot. Kid tried to pull off a miracle jump shot but fouled by missing the one-ball. He reminded himself that Johnny Bishop had always told him to leave such silliness to pros and rank amateurs and vowed not to try any more low-percentage shots during the game.

Hog picked up the cue-ball, placed it behind the head string, and lined up on the one-ball shot, a long bank back to the corner pocket.

"You have cue-ball *in-hand*," Kid said finally ending the silence and the tension of the first game. "You can put it anywhere on the table you want."

"No," Hog answered. "It goes in the *kitchen*. We've always played it that way."

"We're not playing house rules, remember, and BCA general rule one-dash-five says you can place the cue-ball anywhere on the table. Nine Ball doesn't have a specific rule covering *ball-in-hand*, so you can put it anywhere you want."

Hog stood up and listened intensely. "Are you sure? That gives me one hell of an advantage."

"Positive. Do you have a rule book?"

"No."

Kid rolled his eyes. "Why am I not surprised?"

Hog glanced over at Troy, who simply shrugged. Hog smiled and surveyed the loosely dispersed balls. He placed the cue-ball directly behind the one, in perfect alignment with the nine. "Nine in the corner," he called his shot and made it. "Wow-ee," he hollered and laughed. "I'd rather be lucky than good, any ol' day."

That quickly, game one was over. Kid raked the remaining balls to the foot of the table for a new rack, shaking his head in disgust of his performance.

Only three people were allowed in the pool table room during the game: Hog and Kid, of course, and Troy for crowd control. Troy had wanted to call the game off but fearing a riot when the mob—aided and abetted by J.C.—vehemently protested, he decided to let them play. He also accepted their demands to hoot and holler for or against one player or the other when they informed him this wasn't some sissified golf game, and they would "by God" make all the noise they wanted. So, reluctantly, he left the door between the pool table room assessable but nailed a rope across the doorway so spectators could take turns watching the game without physical interruption, and he posted himself at the door.

Word of the pool game spread through the bars and taverns like gold fever. The Last Chance filled with saloon and pool regulars, and more than a few new faces, most of whom wouldn't know which end of a pool cue to hold, but all enthusiastic and curious as to what was going on. Liquor and sandwiches were being sold at record levels. J.C., Dana, and Holly ran the bar to keep the cash flowing. Any old miner who had grubbed the area for riches and gone bust would have been elated thinking they'd finally seen the mother lode, right here in Upland. The neighboring saloons were giving two-to-one odds against Kid to capitalize on the overflow, and all had commissioned a runner to keep them informed of the game's progress.

Hog racked the balls for the second game and Kid broke them with the same ferocious force of the first rack. The balls scattered again, but this time nothing fell. With ease, Hog leaned over the table, stroked the cue and made the one-ball. He got shape on the two, made it, and then tried another low probability shot at a three-ball, nine-ball combination. He missed and left the nine crotched in the corner with the three and cue-ball on a half-ball alignment.

Kid had also been taught that most combos were sucker shots if runouts were possible. He surveyed the table. A couple of clustered balls made any runout, although possible, difficult.

"Sometimes you just have to take the shot," Hog said. "You can't be a weenie all the time."

"Nine in the corner," Kid declared, he'd already made up his mind. He hit the three straight-on using exactly enough left english to throw it into the nine for a perfect combination shot, and the win. "Wow-ee, I'd rather be good than lucky, any oolll day." He gave his best impression of Hog.

Spectators at the doorway cheered and laughed.

Hog smiled. "Oh no, here comes the dreaded taunting." If you can't beat someone, you think you can talk 'em into losin'.""

"You started it."

"But you're just a kid. You're supposed to keep quiet and lose."

"Fat chance." Kid racked the balls for the third game.

"They're sloppy," Hog said, "can you tighten 'em m up?"

Kid re-racked by pressing the balls into the wooden rack as tight as he could. "Is that better?"

"No," Hog complained. "Do you want me to do it?"

"Suit yourself." Kid walked away from the table.

Hog rearranged the balls and re-racked them.

"Why did you do that?" Kid asked.

"Do what?"

"Rearrange the balls."

"I didn't like their position none."

"They were in the same position as the two racks you gave me."

"I gave you fair racks."

"But they weren't that arrangement."

"What difference does it make?"

"If it makes no difference then we'll put them back the way they were. BCA rule two-dash-two says the one-ball goes on the front and the nine-ball goes in the middle. The other balls are to be placed randomly, with no attention to pattern. Yet you gave me a rack with the low balls hidden in the back of the rack and now you want all the low numbers on the apexes."

"The rules don't say I can't rack 'em in that order."

"By racking like that, they're subject to scatter for a better leave, and you know it. You're giving yourself an advantage, however small."

"Okay, okay," Hog said. "I guess I don't need no friggin' rule book with you around. We'll rack 'em like they are from now on. Is that okay with you and BCA?

Kid shrugged. "It's not exactly right, but as long as we do it the same every time, I guess it'll be fair."

Hog's stroke was strong, and the balls scattered perfectly leaving the one and two in the open and making the six in a side pocket. He proceeded to make the one and drew the cue-ball back for a dead two-ball, nine-ball combination, and an easy win.

"Nice shot," Kid said and again raked the balls toward the foot of the table.

Hog racked for game four, setting the balls exactly as he had for the first two games.

"Hog, we agreed," Kid said and looked over at Troy.

"See you're the one who wants to talk," Hog said.

"Just play the game fair, Hog," Troy said, "and let's get this over with."

"Just wanted to see if he was on his toes." Hog laughed and rearranged the balls.

Kid smiled. "Now I have the advantage."

"Just break 'em and we'll see."

When Kid broke, the balls dispersed and the five fell. He had a shot at the one, two, and three, which he easily made, but he couldn't get shape on the four. He played a safety. The safety left only one possible shot: a tricky four-ball bank shot into the nine halfway across the table.

Hog looked the shot over. "I'll play a safety too," he said and leaned over the table. "No, I'll take the shot, nine in the side." He stroked the cue a couple of times, "No, in the corner." He made two more practice strokes. "No, in the side," he said just before striking the cue ball. The four-ball rebounded from the end rail with too much force for the new cushion rubber, careened off the six and into the nine. The nine hammered into the corner pocket. "Damn!" he howled, "I'd rather be lucky than good, any ol' day."

"You are," Kid said.

"I'm what? Lucky?"

"And not good."

"Well I won, didn't I?"

"No, you called it in the side," Kid said.

"I did?"

"You know you did."

"Just wanted to see if you were awake," Hog said as he retrieved the nine-ball and spotted it.

With easy, superb strokes, Kid ran out from there for the win. "Don't worry, I'm awake," he said and grinned.

While Hog and Kid thrashed out ball positioning on Kid's re-rack, Troy walked to the bar. "They're dead even, four games each," he reported.

The crowd cheered and raised their drinks as word spread through the room. A runner broke for the door to inform the other saloons.

Holly meandered from table to table being a pretty, but inefficient waitress. Dana poured drinks at one end of the bar for the few still seated there while most milled about the room discussing the merits and pitfalls of the game of pool. Somewhere in the back of the saloon, someone broke into a singing tribute to the game:

Ya got trouble,
Right here in River City!
With a capital T
And that rhymes with P
And that stands for Pool.
We've surely got trouble!
Right here in River City!

Others joined in another verse and J.C. hummed along to the old *Music Man* song as he leaned on the sink at the end of the bar closest to the pool table room. He dipped whiskey glasses in water, declared them clean, and stacked them for reuse. "Four games each. That's not all bad," he said as Troy approached. "I knew the boy had the nerve."

"I don't know which will prevail, Kid's skill or Hog's luck," Troy said.

"Skill will always overcome luck," J.C. said, "if the games go on long enough. And I figure the refurbished table and new balls will give Kid a slim advantage because that's what he's used to, and Hog isn't."

"You should be in there watching and encouraging," Troy said.

"No way should I be in there, I'm too nervous, and besides, at this point I'd be more distraction than encouragement. Anyway, I talked to Kid this morning, gave him a pep talk, you might say, and he knows the value of everything. He should be fine."

"The town will talk about this game for years, no matter the outcome," Troy said. "Kind of like when you lost to Hog to begin with."

"Must have been insufferable."

"Well, essentially, they talked about what a knucklehead you were. That made it bearable." Troy grinned.

"Ha-ha, funny," J.C. said and smiled, "now get back in there and protect the boy's interest."

Troy walked away then turned back. "Oh, I almost forgot. Do you know a guy named Levi Berry?"

A glass slipped from J.C.'s hand and shattered on the floor. "I've heard of him," he said. "Why? What's up?"

"He may be in town."

"I would suppose he is."

"Is he looking for you?"

"I doubt if we'll see him until the game's over, too many people."

"You'll point him out to me if he shows up?"

"Sounds like a plan."

As Troy returned to the pool table, Hog won an easy fifth game with another improbable shot into the nine-ball, and another outburst about being lucky instead of good. It was as if Troy had never left the room.

Thirty-Three

J.C. kicked the pieces of glass under the sink and poured himself a tall shot of Wild Turkey 101. He moved to the other side of the bar, straddled a stool, and fired up a much-needed Lucky Strike. He knew Kid had won the sixth game because Hog was breaking rack number seven, and he knew that by the sound of the crack of the balls. When he listened carefully, he could detect the subtle differences in each player's break. The sound depended on the amount of english and power driving the cue-ball when it hit the rack, of course. But to J.C., it was more like the balls were talking to him, a memento of life, a keepsake acquired from irrevocable years given to a vocation that had taken all but had given little in exchange—except that sense that the balls would talk to him. He also knew, sure as hell would soon take his soul, that they would no longer listen to him. His days of pool playing brilliance were over. It was like giving up a young wife you'd spent years nurturing and loving, all the while knowing that one day—poof—she'd be gone, gone through no real fault of your own, simply because you were getting old.

"They're halfway," J.C. said when Dana walked up and patted his hand.

"How long can they trade games?" she asked. "When will it be over?"

"Because Hog won the first game, if they continue game for game, he has the advantage to win the match at

206

thirteen. However, if Kid gets hot and wins two in a row the order changes and he takes the advantage and will be subject to win the match. In any case, there won't be a fourteenth game."

"Hog hates to lose, you know. He'll give it all he's got, even playing Kid."

"I wouldn't expect anything less. Though I suppose I should be the one in there playing. I may have put too much responsibility, too much pressure on someone so young."

"Why the hell not?" a voice from behind him said and J.C. looked up. "The kid's holding his own, and I know you've taught him how to handle the stress."

J.C. watched as the small man sporting Western boots, long vest, Stetson Bozeman, and one hell of a blackeye, pushed in close and saddled up to the bar next to him.

"What are you drinking these days?" J.C. asked.

"Coke will do this time," Black Berry answered. "I'm working."

"You heard the man, Dana, Coca-Cola," J.C. said. "And put a little Bacardi in it, I'm buying."

"Why not?" Black Berry looked at Dana and smiled. "I just had a long hike down the mountain from the reservoir and could use a drink. Other than that, it's been a fine day that'll be over before I can get drunk."

J.C. fidgeted with his glass, took a drag of his cigarette. "Did you see the sign hanging over the back bar?" he asked. "It's been hanging there since I was a boy."

Black Berry read the sign aloud: "Firearms must be checked at the bar." He chuckled. "No shit. I checked mine this morning. It's fine."

J.C. glanced toward the pool table room. A crowd had gathered around the door, but Troy wasn't in sight. He turned back to the bar and raised his glass. "Glad to hear it."

"If you even look like you're going to call your brother," Black Berry said, "you'll be dead before you open your mouth, and I'll shoot anybody else who gets in my way."

"Never doubted it for a minute." J.C. put his glass down without taking a sip. "How'd you find me?"

"Your beautiful mother-in-law."

"I should've known she was lying to me."

"I don't think she likes you."

Dana set the Bacardi and Coke in front of Black Berry. "Heck of a shiner," she said.

"Is it that disturbing?"

"Hardly," Holly said. She was now standing behind the bar with Dana. "I think he's kind of cute, even with the shiner."

"She's got my vote." Dana agreed, smiling.

Black Berry grinned at the women. "Thank you, Holly—" he held up his drink in a manner of a toast "—and you too . . . Dana, is it?"

J.C. knocked back the full shot of whiskey, looked at Holly and winked. "You two know each other?"

"He's been here for a while watching Kid play some, and he introduced himself . . . said he was a friend of yours from LA."

"That's nice," J.C. said.

"So," Dana asked, "how'd you get the shiner?"

"Got in the way of something blunt," Black Berry answered and tilted his head toward J.C. "A pool cue most likely."

"If you girls don't mind," J.C. said, "we've got some business to discuss."

The women looked from one man to the other, shrugged, and then walked away talking as if they were best friends.

J.C. watched them leave but spoke to Black Berry. "I guess you've been here for a while?"

"Long enough to know about the game in the back room, and that your skinny ass wife ran off with that hippie freak who hung around the pool hall. Man, you gotta be some kind of a fucking loser to let that mop head run off with your woman."

J.C. tried to get another sip from his empty glass and wished he hadn't sent the girls away so quickly. "Yeah, but I don't know where they went."

"Chicago, I heard. But don't worry your fat ass none; I'm not looking for her, not anymore anyway."

"Just me and the boy?"

"Don't care much about the boy anymore either. Besides you, sixty thousand in cash, that's what I'm looking for. You're the one who put yourself in this position. You're the one who has to pay." Black Berry picked up his drink, rattled the ice around and took a long deliberate sip. He looked at the glass then finished the drink allowing the liquid to flow slowly past his tongue. "Good rum," he said.

"Humph." J.C. let the air escape. "What are you now, some kind of authority of fermented drinks?" He pushed himself off the stool, ambled around the bar, and poured them another full glass.

"I'm a connoisseur of drink, drugs, and sex," Black Berry answered with a broad smile.

"A *connoisseur?* I'm sure," J.C. said. "I'm sure you are."

"You know, I've been through your apartment and your car, couldn't find a damn thing though."

"I was afraid of getting bogged down with the cues so I hocked them before I left L.A." J.C. had already decided if it came to this, he'd take the heat for the cues in hopes Blondie would have a good rest of her life.

"Yeah, I found the cues and shot the turd bucket who bought them," Black Berry said.

"Turd bucket?"

"That's what the big fuck called *me*. Can you imagine . . . turd bucket? I don't even know what the hell it means."

"It fits," J.C. said.

"Yeah, well, never mind that shit, what about the money? It doesn't belong to me, you know. Hell, I was going to return it to its rightful owners the day you made off with it and screwed everything up."

"I find that hard to believe."

"I considered it once, briefly. I really did." Black Berry smiled and tested his fresh Bacardi and Coke. "I mean, at one point I actually thought about giving it back. But then I came to my senses and figured that fucking Mexican wasn't going to let me live either way."

"For some reason, I can't seem to feel sorry for you."

"Screw you and him . . . and his big, bizarre looking brother." Black Berry was already sounding a little tipsy. "And I really don't give a rat's ass how you feel because it's not going to matter much in a little while anyway."

J.C. mulled that for a second. "Kid and I were going to return the money to you, but I changed my mind for the same reason you did . . . figuring you'd still want a piece of my hide no matter what. Even though I'm sure you see the irony, I'd assume there's still no guarantee of me continuing to breathe even if I give it up now?"

Black Berry chuckled. "Yeah, right," he said and took another sip of his drink. "Take a look at what you did to my face, you asshole. And I've been living on nothing more than pain pills and thoughts of payback while chasing you across the goddamn country. I don't see any way you're going to survive this one."

"The girls still think you're cute." J.C. gave him a gaunt smile. "What little modifications I did can't be all bad."

"That seems to be the fact, but it doesn't let you off the hook."

"Figures." J.C. sucked a long pull from his cigarette.

"Damn straight it figures." Black Berry rattled the ice in his glass. "But if you give me my money now, your boy need not know I was even here."

J.C. took a minute. "You'll leave him alone?"

"Look, the more I thought about it the more respect I got for the boy. I mean, the little shit held a gun on me, and I think he might have used it if you hadn't clobbered me."

"Maybe I acted hastily."

"Maybe you did," Black Berry said and smiled, "and look how he's handling himself in there on the pool table. I'm kind of proud of him, so I don't want him to see his old man sprawled out with a hole through his heart. I have some compassion."

"That's nice, and I appreciate it. I really do. So, what do you have in mind for me? I don't want to leave Upland."

"I have a place picked out for you up at the reservoir."

"Nice and peaceful," J.C. said, "I like it up there."

"Nice and peaceful, and you can join some of your neighbors there, as long as you cooperate."

"Will it be painful?"

"Never is."

J.C. raised his eyebrows. "What's left of the money is upstairs."

"What's left of it? What the shit does that mean?" Black Berry hammered the glass onto the bar. "How much is left?"

J.C. hooked his thumbs in the collar of his shirt. "I had some expenses. You didn't expect Kid and me to go without expenses did you. But Christ, I didn't buy a motor home or this establishment or anything like that."

"Just take me to what's left and let's get this over with before my head starts giving me fits." Black Berry gulped down the rest of the rum spiked Coke.

Thirty-Four

The living room was in shambles, the bathroom ransacked, and drawers and beds upturned in the bedrooms. J.C. sighed as he wandered through the upheaval to the dismantled kitchen and poured two tall glasses of Turkey 101.

"If I'd found my money," Black Berry said. "We wouldn't be standing here talking."

"You mean you wouldn't have to face me when you shot me." J.C. offered him the full glass of whiskey.

"Hey, you got me all wrong. I don't mind facing you; I'll take pleasure in it." Black Berry took a healthy swallow of the harsh whiskey and coughed wildly as it burned its way down his gullet. "Damn," he shrieked, "you trying to choke me with this shit?"

"I'm trying to get me drunk. Do you mind?"

Black Berry smiled, held his glass up, and this time took a reasonable sip. "This'll probably interfere with good judgment, but if it'll make it easier on you."

J.C. weaved his way to the living room, kicked the coffee table in alignment with the old sofa, set his drink on it, and sank deep onto the sagging cushions. He unceremoniously fished out a cigarette, set it on fire with a two-inch flame, sucked in a long drag, and casually allowed four perfectly formed smoke rings to puff into the air. At the same time, he leisurely let his free hand slide between the seat cushion and the arm of the sofa.

214

Black Berry righted a wooden dining chair, straddled it facing J.C., took another sip of the abrasive whiskey, coughed again, and smiled patiently. "Not as smooth as rum and Coke," he said, squeaking out the words.

"Whiskey's a man's beverage." J.C. picked up his drink, downed it in a gulp, thumped the empty glass onto the coffee table, and challenged Black Berry to follow suit.

"If I did that I'd pass out," Black Berry said.

"Pussy . . . you come in here all full of shit and vinegar going on about how you're going to shoot me. Yet you're not man enough to drink a shot of whiskey with the condemned man."

"Screw you—" Black Berry hauled his glass up "—to the condemned man then." He swallowed half of what was in his glass, stifled a coughing spasm, and smacked the glass onto the coffee table without spilling a drop of the remaining liquor.

J.C. drew hard on his cigarette, letting his lungs fill; his free hand suddenly stopped its frantic groping beneath the sofa cushion. He'd found what he was looking for and carefully wrapped his fingers around the handle.

"What the hell are you doing?" Black Berry barely able to squeak out the words, "If you're digging around in there for the money—"

J.C. yanked the undersized pistol from the couch and held it within inches of Black Berry's chest. "Now back the hell away from me."

Black Berry stared at the diminutive 22, looked confused for a second then grinned. "I'm such an Idiot. I should've known you were screwing around for a reason. But, as you know, I'm also a gambler by nature, so I'd bet you something large that you didn't have time to chamber a shell in that pissy ass thing."

"Something large? Do you mean my life for yours?"

"That would be it."

"You'd lose, because I damn sure checked the chamber before I hid the pistol in the couch, and if you don't move away from me, I'll prove it right now."

"Even if that's true," Black Berry said, not moving an inch. "I mean, even if you did load it earlier, you wouldn't have cocked it."

J.C.'s eyes darted to the pistol and Black Berry instantly lunged for it. J.C. pulled at the trigger and, when nothing happened, Black Berry yanked it from J.C.'s grip.

"Christ," J.C. said. "Christ O Mighty."

"Now, just get the goddamn money and quit playing games."

All hope drained from J.C.'s face, and his eyes watered. He took another drag from the cigarette and, in a reaction of defiance, flipped the butt at Black Berry. It struck him in the forehead and fell to the floor.

Black Berry swung the undersized pistol and clocked J.C. above his right eye, drawing blood. "I don't know why you're screwing with me, but the cavalry ain't coming."

"I suppose you're right," J.C. said, wiping at the thin trickle of blood running down his cheek. "I was kind of hoping maybe Troy would show up and put an end to this."

"The only thing you're going to do is force me to kill your cop brother and maybe even the boy. Is that what you want?"

"No, I'm done." J.C. let out a defeated sigh.

Black Berry shoved the hand-sized pistol firmly into J.C.'s chest. "Okay then, get the hell up and get my money or I'll shoot you right here with your own gun and then go after the boy. I'm sure he knows where it is."

"Won't be necessary," J.C. said and shoved the pistol aside, pushed himself from the couch, and finally accepting the inevitable led the way to Kid's bedroom.

Pushed against the wall, behind the upturned bed, the backpack hung on the back of a chair. Except for a couple of small straps, it was hidden from view. J.C. retrieved the backpack and held it out. The Joker smiled wildly.

"You are shitting me?" Black Berry said. "I am such an idiot."

"I always thought so."

"Fuck you." Black Berry snatched the backpack. He unzipped it and fumbled through the bills for a second then looked up with wide, glazed eyes, and beamed. "Looks like we have it all . . . man, I was getting worried there for a while."

"Kid's been in charge of it. He's excellent with money, a hell of a lot better than I am. I probably would have left all of it at the blackjack tables in Laughlin if it hadn't been for him."

217

Mose Duane

"I knew I liked that boy," Black Berry said. "He's a money whiz along with being one hell of a good pool player."

"Gonna be a world beater."

"Good for him." Black Berry waved the pistol. "But that don't help you any. Now, since I don't have a vehicle anymore, get your keys and let's take a nice ride up to the reservoir before I change my mind and drop your sorry ass right here for the kid to trip over."

"What, the pretend Porsche thing finally gave out?"

"Yeah, you might say that."

"Go finish your drink first. I hate to see fine whiskey go to waste."

Black Berry smiled broadly, sauntered back to the living room, retrieved his glass, emptied it, and in an extravagant mocking finish, slammed the empty glass onto the table. "And now I hear Canada calling." He laughed boldly.

Thirty-Five

Like the first six games, seven through twelve were indeed split evenly. Hog never attempted a runout, always relying on a play on the nine-ball or making the last couple of balls after Kid missed, always laughing and piping, "I'd rather be lucky than good, any ol' day."

Kid, ignoring Hog's annoying clichéd verbiage, played the best pool of his young life and barely kept up, but did, and won game twelve. He racked the balls as tight as he could for the thirteenth and final game and walked away from the table trying to conceal his trembling fingers. He leaned back on the tall chair at the end of the table, the first time he'd been off his legs since the contest began. Feeling weak, tired, and anxious, the dreaded signs of ever mounting pressure—a loser's demeanor, his dad had told him many times—he closed his eyes and took short, silent breaths. But all he could think about was losing the game. If Hog made the nine on the break, he loses. If Hog runs the rack, he loses. The only chance he had was if Hog missed a shot, any shot.

Hog broke the rack so hard the balls, as a group, rose from the table before scattering. The six-ball again flew into a side pocket before the balls randomly settled onto the immaculate green. The one-ball and two-ball came to rest leaving an easy runout. Hog smiled as he quickly lined up and stroked the one-ball into the other side pocket. The cue-ball careened left, nudged the five and laid up for a straight in two-ball shot. "Maybe I'll just run the rack," he said as he sank the two-ball.

"It'll be your first," Kid replied without opening his eyes. His heart raced wildly.

Hog drew the cue-ball back twelve inches as the three-ball fell, leaving another straight in on the four. Hog made it easily. "Only three balls left," he said.

"Four," Kid said, "the five, seven, eight, and nine."

"How would you know? You're sitting over there frightened shitless with your eyes shut."

"Apparently, I can count better with mine closed than you can with yours open."

"Yeah, okay, only three . . . and the money ball." Hog corrected himself.

"You have to make them all to win," Kid said. "I'm not going to give it to you."

"I didn't expect you would. Anyway, you're as nervous as a cop at a Hell's Angel's rally, I could leave the nine straight in and you'd miss, so I'm not worried."

Kid's eyes popped open. "How's it feel beating a thirteen-year-old?"

"What?"

"Are you going to be proud when you tell everyone you beat a kid?"

"Yeah, I get it, you little fart. You're a bit late to try that crap."

"Crap?"

"I ain't gonna feel sorry for you, so you might as well set there shakin' like a sissy and shut up. Or you can go tell your old man you lost just like he did fifteen years ago, that you're both losers."

"I was just saying—"

"Come on guys, just play," Troy said. "Leave the squabbling for tomorrow."

"Yeah, yeah, I know what you're sayin," Hog replied to Kid as he surveyed the lay of the balls. The five and seven were lined up on one end of the table and the eight and nine on the other. "And it's for damn sure I don't wanna go around braggin' about a thirteen-year-old beatin' me. That's a helluva lot worse than me beatin' him." Hog leaned over the table and played the five-ball into the seven. The seven rolled into the corner pocket. He made the five-ball in the same pocket and drew the cue-ball the length of the table, but it rolled past his intended shape position.

Kid jumped up and watched as Hog weighed his options. There were three: a long bank on the eight-ball while stopping the cue-ball close to the nine, another high-risk combination shot by playing the eight into the nine, or a kiss shot by brushing the eight with the cue-ball, caroming the cue-ball into the nine forcing it into the pocket.

"You're in trouble now," Kid said with a mock smile. "Any good pool player knows to never abandon a shot that's working. You've already made six of seven combination shots, so the odds are in your favor for another one . . . maybe. Then maybe you figure you'd be pushing your luck. Maybe this one will be the one you miss. And the bank shot? Well, we both know you can't bank for crap. That leaves the kiss shot. Maybe you should try it, but it's a delicate, finesse shot, and you're such a klutz. I'm not sure you could pull that off, either."

"Shut the hell up!" Hog yelled, and then tried to calm himself. "Anyway, I could get lucky."

"Luck makes sense, that's how you make most of your shots anyway."

"Just put your skinny ass in that chair and shut the hell up. Damn, just leave me alone for a minute."

Kid raised his eyebrows. He knew Hog was capable of making any shot on the table and then some and wasn't easily riled. He glanced at Troy, shrugged, smiled, and kept talking, "Wouldn't you hate to admit you had to get sloppy lucky just to beat me, like you did to beat my dad?"

"I don't have to get sloppy lucky, and I can be as delicate as anyone." Hog took aim and stroked the cue several times more than usual before striking the cue-ball. It kissed the eight a smidgen too thinly and struck the nine a quarter-ball too solidly. The eight and cue-ball stayed put, but the nine rebounded from the lively cushion toward the opposite corner pocket. "Goddamn it," he yelled and whacked the cue on the table, the first real outburst from either player. "Don't you ever shut up? You are just like him."

"Two shots left," Kid whispered and exhaled slowly to cover his nervousness, "and I don't mind being just like *him*." His hands noticeably shook as he took aim on the eight.

"Look at you," Hog said. "You're so scared you're shakin' like a goddamn rookie."

Kid's stroke was a little jerky, but he knew it, and he also knew that by using the side rail he could play the shot as if he had a six-inch pocket instead of the tight four inches provided by the King Pool Table Company more than a hundred years ago. He gave the cue-ball side english and turned it loose. The Rambow made an unusually loud popping noise and the cue-ball skidded into the eight-ball. The eight hugged the rail for four inches, as if being pulled in by a magnet, and rolled into the corner pocket. The cue-ball followed, but it took a bizarre curving track away from the pocket, rebounded off the end rail, and back toward the center of the table.

"Talk about luck," Hog said.

"Only one shot left," Kid whispered, trying to stay in focus, trying not to let the lucky shot affect his concentration.

"Yep, this is it sure as hell. If you make it, you win the whole caboodle, but if you miss . . ."

Kid was left with two possible shots: a severe cut shot to the corner pocket or a long bank shot to the opposite end of the table. His hand shook only slightly but sweat formed on his forehead. There was no way he could make the cut shot with sweat dripping in his eyes. He took a deep breath to calm himself and leaned over the bank shot.

". . . yes sir, you'll lose it all," Hog continued. He was now glaring from across the table, using an old hustler's trick of standing behind the pocket the shooter was aiming for.

The doorway was packed with bobbing heads, all talking or mouthing their comments. "Come on kid," someone whispered. "You can do it."

Others began softly chanting. "You can do it. You can do it."

Troy closed his eyes.

Just let it happen, Kid recalled his dad telling him a hundred times. It's just a ten-dollar pool shot, no big deal. The old Rambow slid through his fingers, straight and slick, but the stroke had to be solid and when it struck the cue-ball it popped again. This time the wood gave way and splintered at the joint, leaving Kid holding the shaft in one hand and the butt in the other. The cue-ball hit the nine off center, which cocked sideways and spun away from its intended line. Spinning wildly, the nine-ball caught the side rail and came away at an acute angle but continued forward. In bewilderment, Kid raised his head and watched.

"Damn," someone in the doorway said.

Troy's eyes popped open.

"Damn," Hog said and smiled.

"Damn," Kid said.

Thirty-Six

Black Berry and J.C. reentered the saloon from the apartment stairwell, and calmly passed the bar as they walked toward the front door. Black Berry had the backpack slung over his left shoulder and the 22 tucked into his waistband next to his 45, where neither could be seen. He walked at J.C.'s side swaying slightly as the rum and whiskey performed their functions.

Dana and Holly were behind the bar, Dana pouring drinks and Holly had taken over the job of washing glasses. Holly looked up and smiled at J.C. and his L.A. friend.

"If anybody says anything to you, just wave and keep walking," Black Berry said, whispering into J.C.'s ear as they approached the front door. However, the door opened before they got to it and Howard "Jiffy" McGuire staggered in, his revolver hung low on his right hip, and another draped over his left shoulder, holster forward.

Black Berry stopped, stepped backward, and then laughed at the odd-looking combination of filthy clothing and gleaming weaponry. "What the hell are you?" he asked and instinctively moved his hand to his waistband and cocked the 45.

"He screwed my wife," Jiffy pointed a shaky finger at J.C., "and ruined my life forever. I come to shoot him for it. I brought another gun to give him a chance. That's more than he'd do for me."

Black Berry eased his hand back to his side and looked at J.C. with raised eyebrows.

"It was a long time ago." J.C. shrugged. "Like you, the man holds one hell of a grudge."

Black Berry looked at Jiffy and laughed. "You're going to quickdraw *him*? Man, I'd like to see that, and it would solve a big problem for me. But I can't be sure you'd win, and if you didn't, I'd be right back where I'm at now, except he'd have a damn gun. Anyway, why should I let him have all the fun? I've always wanted to be a gunslinger like Josey Wales or somebody." He staggered sideways and stood swaying, hand hovering above his pistol.

Jiffy's jaw dropped.

"Go on draw," Black Berry said.

Jiffy's bewildered eyes glazed over. He stood rock still.

Black Berry pulled the 45 and fired. The shot roared within the confines of the barroom. It hit the holster hanging in front of Jiffy's heart and lodged there, but the force knocked him backward. His eyes rolled upward and with a degrading escape of flatulence, he fainted and collapsed to the floor.

Black Berry raised the gun to his lips and blew over the barrel. "Well, cowboy, I guess now I'm the fastest fucking gun alive." He laughed freely and loudly.

Some in the room, still holding their drinks, simply stopped what they were doing and looked up in dismay, others scrambled for cover on the floor and under tables. Kid was standing in the doorway of the pool table room about to come out when Troy yanked him backward and told him and Hog to duck behind the pool table. He then pulled his weapon and peered around the doorjamb. Holly and Dana had disappeared behind the bar.

"Christ," J.C. said. "Why'd you have to do that?"

"He was going to draw on me, like he was some Billy the Kid or something."

"He was petrified."

Black Berry smiled and placed the barrel of the pistol on J.C.'s chest. "Or maybe he just wasn't fucking fast enough."

"Drop the gun!" Troy yelled from behind the doorjamb of the pool table room.

Black Berry leveled the pistol, whirled, and fired two consecutive shots. One thumped into the trim at the doorjamb, but Troy fell as the other bore through his abdomen, and into the pool table behind him.

"Jesus Christ! Stop shooting!" J.C. flung his arms up and held them there.

"I should drop your fat ass right here." Black Berry pushed J.C. through the front door. "Now let's go for a nice ride before I do just that." They wobbled across the street toward J.C.'s Honda.

On the floor, in front of the pool table, Troy keyed his handheld radio, "Nina . . . I've been shot . . . I'm at the saloon . . ."

227

Thirty-Seven

The air was crisp, clean, and clear, and although the trees were still green, they were taking on the full look of early fall as the wind rustled through heavy branches. Children filled the park, skipping, running, playing, oblivious to J.C. and his crumbling world. Also oblivious were groups of so-called adults scattered about awaiting the outcome of a pool game they had blown well out of proportion to what it actually was; all milling about carnival like with drinks in their hands and, J.C. thought, nothing substantial in their heads.

"It must be a weekend day," J.C. said as he slowly and deliberately ambled into the street.

"What fucking difference does it make?" Black Berry grumbled, grabbed J.C.'s shirt, and began pulling him toward the car.

"You'd think a man would be more aware of his last day on earth." J.C. stopped walking, shrugged, and waved at the crowd.

"It won't matter come tomorrow." Black Berry began waving his pistol to disperse the ambling mob that had now started to migrate toward J.C., smiling at first then suddenly looking mystified as to what was happening. "Get the hell away from me," Black Berry yelled at them then pushed the pistol into J.C.'s stomach. "I don't know why I'm wasting my time with you, but if you don't knock it off and start moving, it'll end right here, right now."

The squall of a siren echoed from somewhere up the street as J.C. picked up his pace. "You know," he said as they made it to the Honda, and he began fumbling through his pockets for the car keys. "I haven't seen the reservoir since me and Troy were the great bass slayers of summers long gone."

Black Berry, now on the passenger's side of the car, aimed the 45 over the top. "It's nice up there, I saw it yesterday. But you'll never see it if you don't quit fucking around because I swear—"

"Okay, okay, we're on our way." J.C. opened the driver's door just as Nina's squad car screeched to a halt across the street, red and blue lights flashing, siren screaming, small groups of onlookers scattering in her wake. She was promptly out of the car squatting behind the door with her handgun drawn and pointed in their vicinity, her eyes darting, scanning. "J.C. what the hell's going on?"

Black Berry instinctively cut loose on her with the last two shots from the 45. One slug passed through the open driver's window, well above her head, shattered the passenger's window, and struck a bystander who instantly fell; some behind him ducked for cover, others scrambled to the downed man's aid.

Simultaneously, a long black limousine squealed around the corner from the opposite direction and pulled up directly in front of Black Berry. "Hey *gringo*," Juan Hernandez yelled and stepped from the limo.

Black Berry drew the tiny 22 and emptied it at the Mexican. One shot punched a small hole in his left shoulder. Two more shots whizzed past his right ear, traveled across the street, and slammed into the wooden sign hanging above the saloon doors.

José now stood with his pistol braced on the roof of the limo, and a single puff of smoke from the silenced S&M instantly blew the side of Black Berry's head away.

Nina had never fired her pistol in the line of duty, and what should have been an automatic response didn't happen. "Police!" she yelled and, wide eyed, looked from one Mexican to the other, her handgun swinging back and forth.

José quickly trained his pistol on her.

"Drop your weapons!" She yelled.

"Officer Troy, he is inside the saloon," José said calmly. "We are United States Marshals and that is the bad guy over there—" he nodded toward the disfigured body sprawled beside J.C.'s Honda "—we were going to follow him out of town and arrest him where it is safe. Then he shot Officer Troy and then you showed up, so we had to change our plan to make sure he wouldn't shoot anyone else."

Nina looked suspicious. "How'd you know Troy was shot?"

"We have a police scanner." José shrugged and grinned large. "We have been working with Officer Troy to get the bad guy. Go ask him yourself; he will vouch for us. Anyway, we have sort of a Mexican standoff here. If you shoot me, Juan will shoot you. If you shoot Juan, I will have to shoot you, and you are much too pretty for such a thing."

Nina stared at José's hefty pistol pointing directly at her head. She raised her hands, carefully stood, and then eased her pistol into its holster. "Okay, I'm with you. Let's not shoot anyone else, all right?"

"Good girl," José said and, as Nina turned toward the saloon, he slid into the limo.

Juan wasted no time. He moved in and kicked the 22 from Black Berry's locked fingers. "Is this it, *Señor*?" he asked J.C. while retrieving the backpack with his right arm. He had no trouble holding a pistol with his damaged left.

J.C. held his hands high and nodded affirmative. "U. S. Marshals my dying ass," he coolly said.

Juan grinned broadly. "My brother, José, he has *grandioso* imagination." He held the backpack up to J.C. The Joker's grotesque face laughing. "It is all here?" He asked.

"And much more," J.C. answered.

"Interest," Juan shrugged.

"Interest," J.C. agreed.

"Your son," Juan said pleasantly, as if nothing much had happened, as if blood wasn't soaking through his silk shirt, "he is *fantástico* pool player. Beat me for *mucho dinero*."

"Gonna be a world beater."

"Who has won the game today?"

"They were even, last I heard."

"Take good care of him, *hombre*," Juan said and jumped into the limo with José. With tires squealing, they sped away.

J.C. gazed across the street to the mob scene at the saloon. To get to Troy, Nina had pushed through the horde of town folk who had shown up because of some misguided belief that something magnificent was taking place; all now looking dazed and confused as they spilled across the sidewalk and onto the street.

Jiffy McGuire then staggered out the door, haggard but alive. Behind him came the beautiful Holly—no doubt Upland's upcoming Rodeo Queen—who had connected with Nina. They were propping a hobbling Troy up, awaiting an ambulance. Next, Hog and Dana came out holding Kid's hand high in the air. They were smiling big and bold as if they'd just won the state lottery, because to them they had, and they were headed for Florida. Kid's nine-ball had slowly, miraculously, hugged the long rail, and, as luck would have it, on its last revolution, dropped into the pocket, giving Kid his victory.

Above it all, hanging above the saloon doors, the wooden sign, for the first time ever steadily and repeatedly oscillated in and out of the overhanging shadows of the building, light then dark flashing: LAST CHANCE . . . LAST CHANCE . . . LAST CHANCE.

J.C. glanced up at the sign and grinned at the fortuitous symbolism. He rapped a pack of cigarettes on the palm of his hand, extracted one, torched it, and his grin broke into a smile as his eye caught the glitter of his pinkie ring.

"Christ," he said, "Christ O Mighty."

Also by Mose Duane

A Rookies Guide to:
    Pool Table Maintenance and Repair
    Buying or Selling a Pool Table
    Playing Winning Pool
    Pool Table Assembly

Novels:
    Last Chance (JC's Last Chance)
    Coyote Stands
    Something Substantial
    The Great Pool Table Heist of Arizona
            (Obama and the Dixie Chicks)
    Bigg Dick: Real Justice
    Pussy Willows: A Bigg Dick Novel

All of Mose Duane's books are available online at amazon.com and kindle, b&n.com and nook, Apple Books, Google Books, Kobo, and major booksellers through Books-in-Print.
    Like him on: Facebook.com/MoseDuane